Simon P. Clark is a children's author, living and working in the UK. Originally from Britain, he has lived and worked in Japan and the USA. His debut novel *Eren* was published in 2014 by Atom.

T0349253

Also by Simon P. Clark

Eren

NOT YET DARK

SIMON P. CLARK

ATOM

First published in Great Britain in 2017 by Atom

1 3 5 7 9 10 8 6 4 2

A CIP catalogue record for this book
is available from the British Library.

ISBN 978-1-4721-1100-5

Printed and bound in Great Britain by
Clays Ltd, St Ives plc

Papers used by Atom are from well-managed forests
and other responsible sources.

Atom
An imprint of
Little, Brown Book Group
Carmelite House
50 Victoria Embankment
London EC4Y 0DZ

An Hachette UK Company
www.hachette.co.uk

www.atombooks.co.uk

*For Ashley, for marrying me even though
she knew this kind of thing would happen.
'You and no other.'*

ZERO

WHEN DID this begin? It's trickier than you'd think.

It could have been in the empty house. That's where the wind roared and the fire first burned. It could have been when she spoke to me, or when she first showed me worlds beyond the world.

Actually, I think it goes back way before all that. It starts before me, before the house and the pier were filled with people, before Baymouth was a town or even a place. It starts with the first life in all the world – whoever, whatever that was – and it starts, if I think about it, when that first life *stopped*.

That, I guess, was Death's first bit-part. That's when it began. Everything else came after.

ONE

'I DON'T SEE why we're doing this,' said Danny. He pulled up his hood, making a show of how cold he was.

'Don't be such a wimp. A bit of wind never hurt anyone.'

'Wow, that's great, *Mum*.'

'Don't call me that.'

'Well then, don't say such mum things.'

He was smiling, at least. Things would be better if he was in a good mood. I put my hands on my hips and raised my voice a bit.

'Well, young man, if you would just *participate* instead of standing there like a *hooligan*—'

'OK, OK!' He put his hands up. 'I give in. I'll play along.'

I wished he wouldn't say that. This was supposed to be fun. He kept on making things difficult.

'You want to be here, right?' I said.

He shrugged. 'Sure.'

''Cause if you've got other things to do—'

'Phil,' he said.

'Philip*pa*.'

'Right, sure. Philip*pa*. I'm fine doing this. Don't stress.'

'I'll try not to. Jerk.'

The wind was stronger here. I tasted the salt of the sea, felt sand rush against my skin. I turned around and punched him on the arm. He laughed and took a step backwards.

'OK, sorry, I didn't mean it. I love how *annoyed* you get.'

'Prick,' I muttered, and I turned back to the house. 'We doing this?'

'Lead on, Boudicca.'

He thought he was being clever. A comeback rattled behind my teeth, but I was too excited to be angry right now. It had taken me weeks to convince him to come, and now we were here, I didn't want a fight.

'So, why this place?' asked Danny.

'Why would you *not*?'

A ripple of sand moved on the pavement beneath us and I followed its movements until the wind died down. We were near the cliff now – near enough that we'd had to push through the metal fencing they'd put up, with its signs and its warnings, and walk along the stretch of land connecting this strange outcrop to the rest of the town. I peered ahead, feeling excited, a little sad, a little nervous. The council had already demolished two of the houses, but this one had been left, caught in some legal loophole, and now it was dying, empty and battered by the sea. Behind me, Danny let out an appreciative whistle.

'I'll give you this, Phil, it's pretty cool.'

'Right?'

'How long's it been like that?'

'Landslide was six years ago. There were three houses, all looking out on the cliff. I guess they shared this driveway. I love it – look, just water on both sides, like you're crossing a moat to a castle. The other two houses got torn down pretty quick. This one—'

'Is it safe?'

'I don't see why it wouldn't be.'

'Um, maybe because of all those signs that said DANGER! And LOOSE ROCKS?'

'Pff.' I waved his words away. 'You scared, Danny?'

'As if.'

'Need your mates with you?'

'I mean, if you want me to call them . . . '

I ignored him and pointed up at the house. 'Those windows weren't broken last time I was here. It's so sad.'

'You went *in*? By yourself?'

'No, I just came to have a look. I like the cliffs. I like the sound of the waves.'

'You're properly mental, you know that?'

I stuck out my tongue, winked. 'When you do it without anyone watching, it's called being artistic.'

'Why would anyone be watching you?'

'No, I just meant—Oh, never mind. We going in?'

He opened his mouth to say something, then shrugged and stuck his hands in his pockets. 'Yeah. Hurry up. I'm freezing.'

'Wimp.'

'Let's just hurry up, eh?'

There was something in his voice that stopped me replying. I never wanted us to fight, but it kept on happening. We'd always been friends – we grew up next door to each other, tapping messages on the wall between our rooms. We went to the same school, went on holiday together – but little by little, things were changing. He had his rugby mates now, and in-jokes I wasn't part of, adventures I wasn't allowed to know about. Danny was an idiot, but he was my best friend.

'Yeah, OK,' I said. 'The front door's been knocked open. Let's go explore!'

'The door's open? And the windows are broken? Sounds like other people have . . .I mean, you're sure it's empty?'

'Yeah, probably. I just want to look inside. I never got to when the house was . . . y'know, alive.'

'Ew, alive? That makes it sound so creepy.'

I put on a fake laugh, a cackle that flew on the wind. 'Come into my cottage, my dear!'

'You are so weird,' he said, and he walked past me, up onto the porch of the house. The wood was splintered and rotting, no match for the salt-wind of the ocean below. The

5

house had been stunning in its time – a perfect, magical place, rich and loved and full of life. Now it made me think of a dried-up insect, a husk, something left behind on the side of the road, still reaching out for the family that had forgotten it. It was tall, white wood covering the front, its roof tiled in deep red. The front door was off centre, its porch stretching out like the hand of a man clinging to the cliff. This house was old, and grand, and utterly broken.

'Oh yeah, this seems safe,' said Danny, but he pushed what was left of the door, and it creaked on its hinges, carving lines in the thin layer of sand already creeping into the dark.

'If this was a sexy teen movie,' he said, 'we would absolutely die in about ten minutes.'

'Good thing you're not a sexy teen, then,' I said.

'Oi!'

'Sorry, I meant, you're *very* sexy. Too sexy to die in the first ten minutes.' I looked at him, pouting a little. 'OK?'

'Whatever.'

'Danny.'

'What?'

'Are you . . . ? Is that a little moustache?'

In a flash he put his hand up to his mouth, covering it and scowling at me.

'Are you growing a *moustache*, Danny?'

'What? No! I just – I just didn't shave today, that's all.'

'Let me look!'

'No! Back off!'

'Whoa! Sorry, man. I'm just kidding. It looks awesome. It does! Really.'

I stifled a laugh and looked away. Danny had his back to me, and when he turned around he still looked annoyed.

'Hey, hot stuff,' I said.

'Don't,' he said, then he grunted. 'Just shut up, Phil. I might grow a moustache. Some of the guys on the team are, so there.'

'Oh, brother,' I said, stepping further into the house. The floorboards shifted under our weight, groaning and creaking. Dust and sand was collecting in the corners. A broken chair lay across the stairs, and glass from the windows shone in the light.

'Wow,' I said. 'This place is awesome.'

'What do you mean, "oh, brother"?'

'Really? You want to keep on that, right now? Look at this place! Is that a stained-glass—'

'Yeah, I want to,' said Danny. He walked over to the stairs, kicking at the broken chair. The wood cracked and splintered, flying into the air. He smirked and looked at me.

'Danny, I didn't mean anything. I just thought ... well, you know. The rugby team. Paul Baxter and Scott Haycott? They're idiots. Everyone knows it.'

'They're my teammates,' said Danny. 'Careful what you say. Teammates look out for each other.'

'Oh, I'm sure they'll never find my body.'

'Why do you have to do that? Why do you have to slag off my mates?'

'I'm not! I'm just saying. And how long have you even been mates? You just—'

'You're jealous, Phil.'

'Philip*pa*,' I said.

'Fine, Philippa! I'm allowed to have other friends.'

We stared at each other, Danny breathing more heavily than normal. He'd raised his voice, and in the empty house the words had echoed and rung in the air.

'I know that,' I said. 'It's fine. I was just teasing.'

'Yeah, well, don't.'

'Fine.'

'Fine.'

I picked up a shard of broken glass from the floor, looked at my reflection, tossed it down again.

'You want to go upstairs?' said Danny.

'I don't know. Probably not safe.'

'Yeah. This is cool, though. Want to go see the kitchen?'

'Sure. Whatever.'

He stepped closer. 'Come on, don't be like that. This is still cool. The other rooms must look out over the water. Want to see?'

The argument that still crackled in the air made everything seem suddenly delicate. My words were glass. They would shatter if I got them wrong.

'Maybe it's not safe,' I said. 'Maybe we should just head home after all.'

'Oh. Yeah. Yeah, you're probably right. Thanks, though. Adventure in a haunted house. Very cool.'

'Yeah.'

We made our way back outside. I tasted salt again, and the chill of the wind made my skin pimple. A seagull was circling high overhead, the screech of its cry fading to a whisper.

'I know you have other friends,' said Danny.

'Gee, thanks.'

'You just . . .I like being with the guys, too.'

'It's fine. Really. You don't need to make things better. We're fine, Danny.'

'Really?' He looked hopeful, and he pulled his hood down, straightening his hair.

'Of course,' I said, punching his arm again. 'You'll need more than that to get rid of me.'

'Awesome. Thanks, Phil.'

'I swear to God, Danny, if you don't stop calling me that—'

'Fine, fine. Philippa. You're the boss.'

'Damn right I am. Best friends, yeah?'

He groaned, but he nodded. 'Best friends.'

We turned to look back at the house, at the crackling paint, the bare earth where its neighbours used to be, the tough grass and the edge of the cliff that tumbled down to the ocean.

'We should come back here. Maybe when it's warmer.'

'If it lasts that long. Landslides, remember?'

'Right, right. Well, for as long as it lasts, eh?'

'Deal.'

'Sweet.'

He smiled, and I smiled with him, and for a moment it was just like it used to be.

Danny cleared his throat. 'I'll see you tomorrow at school,' he said.

'Doing anything after?'

'Practice.'

'Oh, OK. Hope it goes well.'

'Thanks. You staying here?'

'For a bit, yeah. I like it.'

He pulled a face. 'Weirdo. If you're not back by night, I'll avenge your death, probably.'

'It's good to know. Right, go away.'

He laughed and ran his hand through his hair. 'All right. See you tomorrow.'

I watched him as he walked back towards the fence and the road and the town, leaving me with the house.

'Growing a *moustache*,' I muttered, and I kicked at a pebble, watching as it rolled along and fell soundlessly over the drop.

TWO

'IT SOUNDS to me,' said Jess, 'like he's embarrassed about being friends with a girl.'

'You know, I'd figured that much out by myself.'

She raised her eyebrows at me, but she didn't reply.

'I just don't see why *now*,' I said.

'Well . . .'

'What?'

She was smiling. I pulled a face.

'Oh please, great and mature big sister, who is only two years older than me, by the way, won't you share your insight and wisdom?'

'Gladly,' said Jess. She put down her bottle of juice and pointed across the canteen. 'You think that a school is broken into year groups, and it is, yeah, but there's a bigger divide than that. There's kids who are young enough that they're not embarrassed by growing up – the Year Sevens and Eights for sure, some of the Nines, maybe – and then there's those of us who are just at the right age to be embarrassed by everything. Anything. All of it. You've been in the first group, but now – well, Danny at least, he's growing up, and he has the moustache to prove it.'

I snorted into my Pepsi. Jess waited for me to wipe my mouth.

'You're fifteen, Philippa. So's Danny, though I think for guys you tend to have one age for their body and one for their mind.'

'Ew,' I said.

'Fact of life. Try not to think about it.'

I took a bite of my sandwich. 'By your theory,' I said, 'you should be in the "embarrassed by everything" stage – yet here you are, talking like Mum.'

'I'm having lunch with my kid sister before I go to the library to read for an hour. I'm not exactly living the teenage dream, am I?'

'Jess, I—'

'I wasn't looking for sympathy, but thanks. I'm just saying, Danny's going to have to decide for himself if he'll be mates with you while his rugby chums are around.'

'I don't think he wants to be mates even when they aren't around,' I said. I rubbed my face and groaned. 'This is dumb.'

'It'll work out. I like Danny. Plus, we're neighbours. He can only avoid you so much.'

'He won't *avoid* me, Jess.'

She gave me another look. I threw a chip at her head.

'Come on,' she said, 'if you're going to be Johnny No Mates today, we can at least do it together.'

We cleared away our lunch trays, Jess sliding books back into her bag.

'Where do you normally read?' I asked.

'Soft chairs in the library, or the field, if it's sunny.'

'So, chairs it is.'

She glanced out of the window. Grey clouds filled the sky, the first spots of rain already collecting on the glass.

'Right you are.'

The library was packed. We'd left it too late, taking too long to talk over lunch, and the nice chairs were already gone, groups of friends laughing and chatting, their bags piled at their feet.

'Know anywhere else quiet?' I asked.

'Up by Year Eleven lockers, maybe, by the computer rooms.'

'Fine by me.'

We pushed the library doors back open, making our way through the corridors and up a flight of metal stairs. There were already fewer people around, despite the rain outside, and Jess found a spot for us to sit against the wall, out of anyone's way. She pulled a couple of books from her bag.

'Preference?' she said.

'Anything's fine. Thanks for this, Jess.'

'Hey, I'll take what I can get.'

She pulled her knees up, opening the book to a bent-over page. I looked at what she'd given me – some sort of adventure involving a magical stone – and tried to make myself comfortable. After a couple of minutes I had to admit the book was good. I felt Jess next to me, happy, her mind far away, and I heard the sound of the rain outside, getting heavier now, the light diming as the clouds piled up. The sounds of the school faded, the shouts and screams, swearing and pushing getting easier to ignore as I dug into the words. I shifted my weight, turned a page, and—

'Ha, guys, check it out! Phil the Thrill!'

I jerked my head up and looked at the group of boys standing in front of us. I felt a jolt of cold and anger rippled through my stomach. Paul Baxter, Philip Choi, Scott Haycott, Asif Malik . . . and there, behind them, Danny. I looked at him, and he looked away.

'What?' I said. I closed the book and put it on my lap.

'You got any time later? Think I'll still have some energy after practice!'

'What are you—'

'Get stuffed, Baxter,' said Jess. The guys laughed and jostled Paul.

'I'm just being friendly. Your sister should appreciate that!'

'What? Why?'

'Guys, come on,' said Danny. His voice was quiet. He looked at me and then pulled Asif's arm. 'Let's go, eh?'

'What a Romeo,' said Paul, laughing again. 'Dumping her already?'

'She's not— I didn't—'

'Dumping?' I said. 'What are you idiots on about now?'

'Word on the street is you've made a man out of our Danny here. You should be careful! He'll need *some* energy for the match on Friday.'

The others burst into laughter again, and Danny's face was turning redder. 'Guys,' he said, 'drop it. I mean it.'

Jess's mouth was open. I stared at them all, confused and annoyed. 'Made a man out of ... ? What are you ... ?'

Paul Baxter made a gesture, and his mates giggled behind him. Danny pulled at them, trying to move down the corridor. 'I mean it, let's just go, that's not what I—'

'*What?*' I spat. 'Are you mad? That's not – we don't – I would *never*—'

'Never! Hear that, Danny? You need to work out more.'

'Piss off,' said Jess, standing up and taking a step towards Paul. He smirked at her and took a step back.

'I'm just sharing stories from the changing rooms. Isn't it good to know what's being said?'

'What's being said by *you*, you twat,' said Jess.

'Danny, why would they—' I started, but the guys were already crowding around him, punching and laughing. I heard him shouting over them all, 'I never said that! I never!'

'Word on the street, Philippa the Thrillipa!' said Paul Baxter, and he was already moving away when Jess reached out and shoved him.

'Get lost,' she said, and she turned back to me. 'Come on, let's go. The rugger buggers need some time alone.'

'Oooh!' said the boys.

'Guys, I never said that,' Danny was shouting. 'It was just jokes— you just said—'

'Come on,' said Jess again, and she took my hand, pulling me away.

'Those *pricks*. They just like getting people to respond! I should have done more than push him, I should have—'

'Jess.'

'Well, they're just idiots!'

'They didn't say anything about you.'

'But you're my sister! And Paul *knows* it's all lies, but you know now he's going to go around and—'

'I don't care.'

'But it's not—'

'Jess,' I said. She stopped pacing. She looked at me and her shoulders sagged.

'Oh, Phil,' she said. 'I'm sorry.'

'Danny wouldn't have said those things, right?'

'No. The others are just making it up.'

'Why, though?'

'Because between them they've got about as much chance of getting with a girl as I have of getting a rugby ball up their asses, which believe me, I—'

'Jess!'

'Well, they deserve it.'

'They're just boys.'

She threw up her hands. 'Don't say that! It's not OK to be a knob just because you have one. They're not just boys, they're idiots. You see that, right?'

I smiled. 'Is this you in protective big sister mode? They should be afraid.'

'Yeah, they should!'

She sat down next to me, putting her arm around my shoulder. 'Sorry. This is your thing, not mine. You and Danny going to be OK?'

'We always are. Best friends, you know.'

'Right. Well, you let me know – 'cause I know where to get a rugby ball, and with a bit of force ... '

'You, big sister, can be surprisingly scary sometimes.'

She squeezed my shoulder and gave a small bow.

'Come on, lunch is over. Time to get to class.'

'An educator, too. Mum will be so proud of you.'

The rest of the day did not go well. I felt like people were whispering, looking at me, smiling behind their hands, laughing behind my back. For the first time, I was glad I didn't have classes with Danny. I sat at the back of geography, trying to remember the names of extinct volcanoes. I coloured in a map of tectonic plates and watched the clouds outside, counting the minutes till school was over.

'Is it true you and Danny Perkins are dating?'

I looked up. Two of the girls sitting in front of me – Vicky Lane and Sarah O'Halligan – had turned round in their seats. They watched me, eyebrows raised, and then Vicky said again, her voice a harsh whisper, 'Are you two, like, going out?'

'No we're not,' I said. 'We're just friends.'

'Oh. Just friends, now? Too bad. He's cute, right?'

'We've always been friends,' I said.

'Well, yeah, we know,' said Sarah. 'But will you be now that you've ... you know?'

I closed my eyes, clenching my fingernails into my palm. 'We never did!' I said. The people nearest us turned to stare. Mr Allcock looked up from his desk.

'Settle down,' he said.

'We didn't do anything. We're just friends,' I said. 'Paul Baxter made it up.'

'Oh,' said Vicky. 'Oh, OK. So Danny's single, then?'

'I don't know. I'm not—'

'His girlfriend, yeah, got it. Thanks.'

They turned away, whispering to each other. I stared at them, looked around the room, desperate for someone to explain to, someone who would tell me how mad this all was.

18

'He can tackle me!' said Vicky, and the girls started laughing.

'Oh, ew, ew, ew,' I said, and I shut my eyes.

'Girls,' said Mr Allcock.

I looked down at my paper, making myself think about dead volcanoes.

By the time the bell rang for the end of the day, the rain had stopped and the clouds had started moving again. Jess ran up beside me as I walked out of the school gates, an umbrella clutched in her hand. 'Walk home together?' she said.

'Don't you have band?'

'Not today. And I thought you might need this, you know, if it rains again.'

'Um, thanks. That's sweet.'

We set off together, crossing over and walking down the hill into town.

'So,' said Jess. 'Um.'

'Yes, other people heard and asked me. No, I'm not mad at Danny.'

'I wasn't going to—'

'Yeah?'

'Oh, all right. So sue me.'

We kept walking. The puddles in the road shone rainbow colours with grease and oil.

'Won't Mum and Dad wonder why you didn't go to band?' I asked.

'I'll tell them I didn't feel well.'

'Lying to our parents!' I said, gasping in shock, my hand on my heart. 'Why, Jessica Ravenhurst, whatever next? Mingling with the lower orders?'

'Oh, I should hope so,' she said, and she laughed, swinging the umbrella in circles. We kept walking, past shops and offices, the old bus station, until the buildings turned into houses, the noise fading away, and we headed away from the main road.

'You know the houses out by Winterbourne Farm?' I said.

'The ones that fell down?'

'Yeah. Did you ever see them, y'know, before the cliff fell?'

She bit her lip, kicking at a can on the pavement. 'I think once I went up there trick or treating. I don't really remember. Why?'

'No reason. Just seems a shame, those big houses, all broken down.'

'They must have had great views,' said Jess. 'Right out over the sea. Imagine your whole house falling down into the water, though. Yikes.'

'Well, the houses didn't fall, did they? The ground was just loose so they *could* have fallen.'

The sun had started to shine now. I felt warmth on my face. The light glinted off puddles, dancing as the water moved in the wind. Distant, like a drum beat, the sound of waves thrummed through the air.

'Is this for a project or something?' asked Jess.

'Oh, uh, yeah. Land erosion. Geography.'

'Bleh.' She pulled a face. 'I always liked history better.'

'Geek.'

'Well, I'm no Phil the Thrill, but—Hey!'

I'd pushed her into a passing bush. She laughed, brushing herself off, and sighed.

'We'll sort them out,' she said.

'They'll never find the bodies.'

It only took five more minutes to get to our street. We were walking towards the coast, and the cold wind, fresh from the Atlantic, stung our faces, even with the sun.

'What do you want for tea?' asked Jess. 'I fancy fish and—Oh.'

She stopped, looking ahead to our house. Outside, leaning against the wall, their bikes piled on the pavement, Danny's teammates were laughing, passing around a cigarette.

'Not *here*,' said Jess. 'Haven't they—'

'They must be with Danny,' I said. 'It's fine. Come on.'

It only took a few more steps for them to notice us. They elbowed each other, nodded their heads, and then Paul Baxter stood up straight, opening his arms wide.

'Hey, girls! Missing Danny already?'

'Move it,' said Jess.

'This is my house, moron,' I said.

Paul grinned. 'Easy access, eh?'

'Get stuffed.'

'I'll leave that to Danny boy.'

'Like I would!' I spat.

'Phil, don't,' said Jess. 'Come on, let's just—'

'He's a fine, upstanding gent,' said Asif Malik. You could see where he'd started to pluck his eyebrows. I wondered if I should tell him.

'Where is he?' said Jess.

'He'll be out in a minute. His dad's got beers.'

'I swear, you couldn't make this up,' said Jess.

Paul stepped forward. 'You have a problem?'

'You're a bunch of greasy kids on bikes,' I said. 'Sharing a smoke and *trying* to grow beards isn't going to help. You're just a baby, Paul Baxter.'

'Oh yeah?'

I took a step forward. 'And Danny's not so great,' I said airily. 'A fuzzy lip and his *dad's* beers don't make him much of a catch, eh? So, like I said, get stuffed.'

For a second, he didn't say anything. He was angry, I could tell, and he wanted to do something in front of his mates. Then, his eyes flickered to the house, and his face split into a grin.

'Hear that, Danny? Wow. She has a good point. Maybe you're not right for the team?'

I groaned, turning around to see Danny. He was standing in the doorway to his house, three cans of beer in his hands, watching us with a blank expression.

'Danny,' I said, 'that's not what I—'

'That's got to hurt,' said Paul, 'hearing that from the one girl in school you might have had a chance with!'

For a few seconds Danny didn't move, but then he shook his head, blinking a few times. 'What?' he said.

'You know what?' said Jess, raising her voice. 'I'm done with this. You lot, get lost or I'll call the cops. Stealing beer and underage smoking. Let's see what your parents all think.'

'Jess, don't.'

It was Danny, dropping the beers and running forward. 'Just leave it, OK?' he said.

'Danny, do you *seriously* think that—'

'Uh oh, Mummy's here,' said Paul.

'Shut up,' said Danny. 'You don't know what you're talking about.'

Paul's smile flicked off and on again. 'Switching sides, Danny? Hoping for some favours after all?'

'Shut up, Baxter. We all know you tried to get off with Kasia Nowak and she shot you down. Don't act so tough, eh?'

Asif and Scott laughed. Paul straightened up, shrugged. 'Man, she gave me blue balls. Whatever, I don't care.'

'I kind of think you do,' said Jess. She leaned closer. 'Now get stuffed, yeah? You and your balls can jog on.'

I glanced at Danny. He looked nervous, angry, like everything was going wrong.

Paul cocked his head, looked at his mates, spat on the ground. 'Whatever,' he said. 'I'm out of here. Come on, lads. We'll leave the ladies. Maybe Danny doesn't want to be on the team, eh?'

Danny moved forward. 'Guys—' he said.

Paul pulled his bike up and jumped on.

'Have fun being one of the girls, Danielle.'

'No, wait, I don't— that's not—'

'Sort it out, Perkins,' said Scott, and then they were off, laughing and shouting, calling to each other, their bikes throwing up dust, leaving us behind. The air felt thick with silence.

'They're like a cartoon,' said Jess. She ran her fingers through her hair. 'You coming in?'

I nodded. My shoulders felt tense. 'In a sec. Danny, what the *hell*?'

The words poured out of him like water from a shattered well. 'I never said anything! We were just joking around, talking about the girls in school, and of course they know we're friends, and they were just asking, just joking, I never said that we— that you and I—' He turned away, kicking at the wall, grunting in frustration. 'It's just a bit of fun,' he said.

'Oh. Fun. OK.'

'Oh, don't say it like that. I don't have to explain.'

'I didn't say you did! But those guys are *colossal* twats. You know that, right?'

He groaned again, burying his face in his hands. 'Thanks for the tip.' He looked up at me. 'Y'know, maybe they wouldn't have been like that if you didn't have to show up and—'

'*Show up?*' This—' I jerked my finger towards my house '—is where I live, remember?'

'How could I forget?'

Jess coughed, taking a few steps towards the house. 'So, I'm just going to . . . go. Bye, Danny.'

Danny looked at her and grunted.

'Awesome. See you later.'

I'd never seen Danny so angry before. I watched as he picked up a stone from the garden and smashed it against the road.

'That seems helpful,' I said.

'Whatever.'

We stared at each other, an angry silence clouding the air. I cleared my throat.

'Well, now they're gone—'

'I'm allowed to have other friends,' said Danny. His voice was quiet and steady.

'I never said you couldn't!'

'Then why do you make such a fuss about the guys in the team?'

'Because of what they say to me! We're meant to be best friends, and then you won't even stick up for me?'

He spat on the pavement. 'I did just now, didn't I? Paul looked right pissed off. He'll have me for that.'

'And what about the changing room? When I'm not there? You stand up for me then?'

'I do,' he said, 'sometimes. But it's just a bit of fun, the things they say, and all the other guys do it, Phil.'

'Well, they shouldn't.'

'Well, they do!'

'Well, they shouldn't!' I said again, raising my voice. Danny was glaring at me, his face dark with anger.

'Did you hear what Paul said about the team?' he said.

'He can't actually do that. The teachers are the ones who—'

'But that's not how it really works. I like rugby. I like the guys. That's what I mean, you don't even care that I like them, you just want to keep me like you, with no one else, and—'

'What?' I hissed. 'What? How can you say that?'

'Because it's true, isn't it?'

'Oh, like you're so popular? Like anyone else has come to your birthday parties beside me?'

I'd struck a nerve. He clenched his fists, opening and shutting his mouth. I smiled.

'And your moustache looks stupid,' I said.

It was like popping a balloon. Whatever had been holding Danny back was gone. His voice was raw and angry. 'Screw you, Phil! You love saying we're best friends like some bloody

26

stupid kid, but you know what? You're a shit friend. Why don't you piss off?'

Everything felt wrong. My ears were filled with the sound of sparks. 'Me? Why should I—'

'Yeah, you! Piss off and be by yourself. You're good at that, right? You should get used to it!'

We faced each other, me and him, and too many words hung between us.

'Fine,' I said, trying to sound calm. I threw my bag down inside the front garden and started walking away. 'Fine, I'll just get out of your manly hair, then!'

I was running now, as fast as I could.

'Phil, wait!'

I heard Danny calling after me, but I was *furious* with him, and with Paul Baxter, and with school, and the anger made me stronger. I ran, my lungs hurting, my feet pounding and aching, and soon I'd left Danny behind, and no one was shouting anything.

I don't know why I chose it. I wanted to be alone, and you can't get more alone than an empty house, on an empty street, with nothing but ocean touching the horizon. It was easy to slip through the fences again, and now I knew the door was open and the floor was solid, I ran into the empty house before I'd even stopped for breath. This time I was bolder. I picked up the chair that covered the foot of the stairs and threw it to the side. I could hear my own heartbeat drumming in my ears, but I was angry still, so angry, and I didn't care what happened. I took hold of the banister and moved as quickly as I could, wincing at the creak and groan of the wood, racing to the top.

'Not so useless after all, eh?' I said to the house, and I laughed, wiping the sweat from my forehead. There were four rooms up here. One was the old bathroom, the porcelain sink shattered and filthy. Opposite it, at the other end of the hallway, a smaller room, completely empty, with mould growing up the wallpaper. The other two rooms were larger, with wardrobes built in, one with an old iron bed frame, a few pictures still hanging on the wall. I wondered why the owners hadn't taken these – did they miss them? Did they have copies? I tried to imagine leaving a house to die, knowing that it had been mine. I shivered, and moved to the window. These were the rooms at the back of the house, the glass still intact, the white-tipped waves spreading out for mile after mile. I smiled, watching the water break on itself. It was already starting to get dark. The ocean sparkled and glistened as it moved, and I felt my head clearing, my heart slowing.

How had things got so complicated? It had never been like this, all this fighting, all this hiding, all these secrets. Me and Danny against the world – that was how it worked. We didn't care about anyone else 'cause we didn't need anyone else. We grew up together, played together. It shouldn't matter that he was a boy, that I was a girl. It wasn't weird. It never had been before.

I remembered last summer, the end of the holidays, when the circus had come to Baymouth, all noise and smoke and cheering crowds. We'd gone, of course, just the two of us, promising our parents not to get into trouble, not to let these madmen snatch us away. We were stupid and excited and hyped up on sweets. Danny made me buy him candyfloss.

'It's magic!' he said.

'It's literally just food colouring and sugar.'

'The size of your head! And then it melts – mmm. Come on, Phil, get us one, and I'll get you back later.'

I sighed, pretended I was annoyed, but we both grinned as we watched the guy making them, swirling the sticks round and round as the candyfloss grew, and it really was like a spell.

'You eat that and you'll be sick on the dodgems!' I said. Danny ripped a piece of his off and threw it at me, and I shrieked, jumping away. He pulled a face and wiped his hand on his jeans.

'Ew. So sticky.'

'Good one, Einstein.'

Around us the circus was a maze of people and colour and mayhem. We wandered through the crowd, eyes wide, counting our money. 'Check out the jugglers!' said Danny, laughing. He grabbed my shoulder, turned me around to see. A flash of fire lit up the crowd and we felt the heat on our faces. 'Whoa!'

'Come on,' I said, 'you going to win me a teddy bear?'

'Let's do one with guns,' he said. 'You know, knock over the ducks. I'm an ace shot.'

I laughed. 'As if! When have you ever held a gun?'

'Whatever. I've seen movies, it's all the same. You want this teddy?'

'I want the teddy.'

'Well then, m'lady,' he said, touching an invisible hat, 'let's see about this here shootin', shall we?'

The crowd moved again and the air smelled of popcorn and oil. 'Here,' I said, 'see? Shoot five targets, win a prize. Let's do it!'

The night air was warm, the last specks of summer flowing away on the wind out to sea. Electric lights hung from tents, from poles, from everywhere.

'I'll win you one,' said Danny, 'if you'll win me one. Seems fair, really.' He wiped his mouth with the back of his sleeve.

'What if I win one and keep it myself?' I said.

'Then you'll get two, 'cause I'm a man of my word, but then you'll feel pretty bad, and you'll look weird.'

Some of the kids from school were around, and we waved to them, beaming, shouting over the noise and the rush. 'We're going to win the bears!' we said. 'Four shots and you get a bear!'

And we laughed, and it was just fun, and we both reached for our money, not really caring if we'd make the shots.

Now, in this empty house, I felt those memories echo like old music.

I pulled out my phone. I had plenty of pictures of Danny and me – hanging out by the beach, messing around in the park with kids from school, and whole days spent at home, watching TV, playing games. It was darker now in the house and the glow of the screen made the pictures look garish and stupid, a make-believe world that was real right until it slipped away without me noticing.

'Bloody emo,' I muttered. I flicked through more pictures, of me and Mum and Dad, of me and Jess, of all of us on a trip to Edinburgh, one to Paris, a weekend in Lisbon. I wanted that feeling back. In the house, in that moment, the world was a pretty dark place.

I must have stood there for half an hour, swiping, swiping, looking at photos from years ago, always going backwards. Danny was there, his goofy grin, his terrible haircut, his cheeks getting chubbier as we got younger. From where I was standing you could see the sweep of the sea, its silver-blue brilliance, the froth of far-off waves. Things that were far away and out of reach. If I'd been feeling any worse I might have written a terrible poem.

The waves hummed and whispered and I shivered at the wind. Danny's words rang through my head. I shouldn't have run away like that. God, what was I thinking? I looked so stupid, and how did that help? I was cold, I was angry, and – I winced as I thought the word – I was alone.

'I'm an idiot,' I said.

'You are,' said a voice in my ear.

THREE

D ANNY WAS bent over laughing, which was lucky, because it made him harder to punch.

'Don't you *ever* do that again!' I said. 'I almost had a heart attack! I could have killed you!'

'Killed me with your scream, you mean?'

'I didn't scream, I yelled, which is exactly what you would do, you jerk!'

He stood up, wiping his eyes, and held up his hands. 'OK, OK, I'm done. Damn, Phil, didn't you hear me calling you? My bike wouldn't fit through the fence, and I didn't want to leave it, so I had to go back.'

I took a few deep breaths, trying to calm down. 'You followed me,' I said.

'Well, yeah. I felt bad. I was just annoyed. I didn't mean any of that. The lads can be ... '

I waited, not wanting to make it easy for him.

'I mean, they can be idiots, yeah,' he said.

'*Lying* idiots.'

'Lying idiots.'

'Jess has plans for them involving a rugby ball and some places,' I said. Danny winced and nodded.

'She'd probably do it, too,' he said. He walked to the window, looking out at the water and the clouds. Our shoulders were touching. I tried to think what to say.

'I wasn't crying,' I said.

'I know.'

'I was just annoyed.'

'I didn't mean it,' he said again. 'I'm sorry.'

The waves hissed and bubbled in the fading light.

'And,' said Danny, 'how about you?'

'Me?'

He sniffed, but it had to be from the cold. 'Are you sorry?'

I nudged him. 'Of course. Even though I was right, for the record.'

'Oh. Sure. OK.'

He flicked his head at the endless ocean.

'Pretty neat. I guess you're right, it's a shame these houses are goners.'

'I'm sorry, I'm what?'

'Oh, come on, Philippa. You were *right*. You're always right.'

'I am,' I said. 'Thank you.'

He nodded, smiling, and cleared his throat.

'This could be our hideout,' he said. 'When it's not so bloody cold.'

'For smuggling?'

'Sure. We could have a den.'

'Ooh,' I said, 'I've never had a den. Very Enid Blyton. We could thwart ne'er-do-wells.'

'Uh,' said Danny, 'sure. Or just have parties. Like, if it's still here for Halloween.'

'Very spooky,' I said, 'and we'd definitely get in trouble.'

We stared at the water as the dark grew thicker. It was nice, the calm after the storm, like we'd stepped back to who we used to be.

'Danny,' I said.

'Hmm?'

'We can't let people make us angry. At each other, I mean. I know it's weird, sometimes, and people make jokes, I know they do—'

'It's not *too* weird.'

I nudged him. 'No, it is, it's OK to say. Still, I hope—'

'I'll tell the boys to back off. You matter more than them. You're my mate.'

There were lights out at sea, flashing on and off. I watched them blink, an impossible mystery, something so far away it might as well have been another world.

'Good. Thanks. And if Paul Baxter wants to—'

'You don't need to worry about him,' said Danny. He turned to face me. 'Here, you want to know something that'll make it easier to deal with him?'

I straightened up. 'Sure.'

'Right. So, the thing is ... ' He hesitated, looked out of the window again.

'What? What's the thing?'

'I shouldn't really, but this is because I feel bad for shouting at you. Let's just say that for all his bragging Paul really doesn't have a lot going on ... down there.'

For a moment I stared at him, at the twitch as his mouth crept into a smile. Then, 'What? Oh my God! Danny, why would you ...? Oh my God!'

He burst out laughing. I gasped, started giggling, pushed him.

'I don't need to know that!'

'Makes you feel better, though, right?'

'Oh, ew!'

'So if you're ever annoyed at him, just think—'

'No, stop, stop!'

We were laughing so much it hurt, gasping for breaths of the freezing air. Danny slumped down, wiping his eyes, shushing me, calling me over.

'You can't ever tell anyone I said that,' he said. 'Oh God, I shouldn't have said, but he was such a dick to you.'

'Don't say dick!' I said, and we were laughing harder now, two lunatics in the attic. Danny's face was flushed.

'Just don't say anything,' he said, wiping his eyes again with the back of his sleeve. 'It's definitely against the code of the changing rooms. They'd probably straight up murder me for talking.'

'I can't believe you. Seriously, Danny, that's so messed up.'

He was giggling now, and I sat down next to him.

'Oh, there's an image it'll take years of therapy to get rid of,' I muttered.

'Speak for yourself – I had to look at the real thing.'

I was laughing so hard my sides hurt, my jaw hurt, and everything was good, there with Danny in the house on the cliff.

I don't know how long we sat there talking, chatting about nothing, shivering and refusing to move. It felt like something was special, that the moment was like a spider's web – if we tried to move it, it would break. Outside the waves rolled on, as they always had and always would. Finally we fell into silence, and Danny got out his phone, and with a single shattering jolt we were reconnected to the world.

'Message from Choi,' he said. 'Just checking in.'

I shivered and stepped over to the window again. 'OK,' I said, 'let's go back. Thanks for coming here. I appreciate it.'

He shrugged. 'No worries. Didn't want you getting murdered or something. I'd feel bad and it'd look terrible in the papers.'

'Real gent, you are.'

He put his phone away. 'I'm an idiot, but that's fine with me.'

We headed back to the landing, down the rickety stairs,

me rubbing my hand along the smooth wood. Danny turned to say something and froze.

'Crap,' he hissed, and he hurried down ahead of me.

There were voices outside, muffled but getting louder, men and women, heading for the house.

'Crap,' he said again. 'Is it illegal to trespass?'

'I think so.'

He swore under his breath. 'We have to hide!'

'What? Where would we—'

Danny grabbed my arm, pulling me from the main room and into the old kitchen. He looked around wildly, and then pointed to the other end of the room. Along both walls, from the floor to waist height, built-in cupboards lay covered in dust. Danny rushed forward, pushing me to the left and ducking right.

'Hide behind the end!' he hissed.

'But what if they actually come *into* the kitchen?'

He nodded towards the back door, halfway between our two hiding places. 'That ought to give in with one good kick. So—'

'Duck!' I whispered, and with a groan and a scrape, the front door was pushed open, and the strangers entered the house. I heard a woman's voice first, then a second, and then men, all talking at once in whispers and mumbles. I looked across to Danny, trying not to move. His back was pushed against the end of the cabinets, his knees pressed to his chest, his eyes wide.

'And you're sure?' someone said.

'I told you, it's empty. Did you see any cars? There's no one here. It's perfect.'

Someone scoffed. 'Just because there're no cars . . . '

'I'll check upstairs,' said a woman. 'Patty, you come with me.'

'The gentlemen can double-check down here,' said someone, their voice louder than the others. 'Richard, George, you have a look back down the drive, make sure we weren't followed, hmm?'

'Right you are.' There was movement, the sound of feet on wood, whispers and echoes.

The woman spoke again. 'So, Patty, upstairs?'

We heard feet on the stairs, muffled and steady, and then they were above us, clomping and echoing. They moved from room to room, still talking, their words too faded to hear.

'Thinks she's in charge, does that one,' said a man. He coughed, and then cleared his throat. 'George, you look over there, and I'll . . . Ah, the kitchen. Yes.'

Another man spoke, his voice thick with an accent I couldn't place. 'She is in charge. Don't forget.'

'Oh, how could I? How could I? Kitchen's here, look.'

Danny's face had gone whiter. He raised a finger to his lips and shook his head. I nodded, pulling myself into a tighter ball, trying to hide in the cramped space between the wall and the cupboards. There was someone in the kitchen doorway now. I heard him muttering, heard the rustle of his jacket, and then his hand tapping on the kitchen bench. Danny jumped but didn't make a sound.

'What a waste,' said the man in the doorway. He was moving closer. I held my breath.

'Just ghosts now, eh?' said someone else.

'What's that, Cully?' said one of the women. She'd made her way back downstairs, and she sounded like she was coming closer.

'Oh, nothing. Just lamenting the way this poor house is being treated.'

'Nostalgia, is it?'

They were moving away. I took a slow, shuddering breath, my legs starting to cramp up.

'A passing fancy. There's no one here. We should begin. I don't like being so . . . exposed.'

One of the men made a scoffing noise. 'I've been here every evening for more than a week. I've never seen a soul. It's perfectly empty. There's no risk.' There was the sound of a boot scraping over the floor. 'Grant you, it's not exactly salubrious, but—'

'We need it,' said someone else, and their voice reminded me of a teacher, someone used to explaining things. 'Wood that stands by water. That's part of it. Wood by water. It won't work otherwise.'

'Plus,' said another voice, chuckling slightly, 'no one will hear us out here.'

'The space is ideal,' said the woman in charge.

The man sounded happy. 'Quite right, Susan.'

When she answered, the woman's voice was cold, almost brittle. 'I know, Cully. Come on.'

They'd left the kitchen now, back into the main room. There was no way to get to the front door, but if we were quiet, and it opened without too much fuss, we might be able to get out the back, to run around and away.

'Friends,' said the woman called Susan. My skin prickled, my mouth dry. 'The time has come. We all know why we're here. We all know what we're here to do. We have ... we have lost so much, and now we will take them back.'

There were murmurs of agreement, and the sound of shuffled feet. Danny pulled a face, confused, still scared. *We have to go*, he mouthed.

'How?' I whispered, and he sighed, shifting on the floor.

'I know that I do not ... do not speak often of my own loss,' said Susan, 'but it seems right that here, before so many things change, I should share a little more of my story.'

'You don't have to,' said another woman, Patty, they'd said she'd sounded old – I wanted to see. My whole body felt numb.

'Thank you,' said Susan, 'but it's right, I think. We go in to this with our eyes wide open, isn't that right?'

'Quite right,' said one of the men. The group murmured their agreement.

The woman took a deep breath, let it out through her nostrils. Around us the house was silent.

41

'Peter was killed in a car crash. I don't think he felt much. The paramedics said he was killed instantly, but that could have just been a kindness. I was driving. We had been – that is, I had been drinking. Not a lot. Not too much. The crash was caused by the other driver, some young fool ignoring the lights. I've no doubt about that. I was not to blame. But it . . . preys on you. And Peter is dead. Because of some stupid mistake and a few seconds of scraping metal and . . . what? That's it? He's gone. No!'

The last word rang through the house. I saw Danny flinch. His eyes were wide.

'I just . . . don't accept it. I can't. I couldn't. No,' said Susan. 'It isn't right – it is wrong – and so I knew I had to fix it. Why should Peter die, and not that young idiot, that driver who walked away, who gets to have his life, his idiotic, wasted life, with no regrets, no scars, no damage? No. I can't accept that – as I know you cannot.'

'Noah – my boy,' said one of the men. 'Illness. A few months. Snuffed out, like he was never even there.'

'My wife,' said Cully. 'She – she was mugged. Hit her head. Murder, plain and simple. Jail's too good. Jail's too good.'

The room was filled with the group's chatter, names they called out, the sound of sniffing, of silent tears.

'Devesh.'

'Siobhan.'

'Veronica, my friend.'

'Mother.'

'Timmy. He was only four.'

Susan cleared her throat, and when she spoke, there was something darker in her voice, something dangerous, wild, an anger that had turned into something worse.

'Death,' she said. 'Death. What is that? An idea, a monster, an unstoppable force? A Grim Reaper with his hands of bone and his unseeing eyes and his heartless chest? Death is final. Isn't that what they say? Ha! And what do we say to that? What do we, the Society, say to that?'

'No more!' shouted the others. 'No more! No more!'

'No more!' said Susan. I could hear her breathing. 'No more to that. Death has been doing his dirty work unchecked for too long. Taking what he wants? Pah! Taking your loved ones? Taking mine? Taking Peter?' She paused. 'No,' she went on. 'No. It's time for us to be the masters. It's time for our pain to matter. It is time for us to act and to put this world *back* on track.'

Danny stared at me, his eyes wide.

Susan raised her voice. 'Then we all agree, don't we? This is the right thing to do. It's meant to happen. Think of the power, friends! Think of the works we can do when this – this gift – is ours!'

'Years, it's taken,' said one of the men. 'Thought it might be a bit grander, but still.'

'This house is empty and quiet,' said someone else. 'We need the wood and the space. You get that, don't you?'

Susan cleared her throat and the group fell into silence. 'The Society exists for one purpose,' she said. 'We have worked and bled and been laughed at, and now – now we reap our reward, dear friends.'

Danny shifted his weight again, his jaw tense and clenched.

'We're all equal here,' Susan continued, 'and as we all rise, we all fall. Don't forget that, ladies and gentlemen. The path that led us here involved sacrifice. We cannot shy away from this. We have . . . we have killed for this book, and we all share in that.'

A tiny gasp spat from my lips. Danny winced, but no one else moved. The house was silent for one heartbeat, two, three. Then –

'We did what had to be done,' said Cully. His voice had lost some of its power. 'To keep the secrets. To keep the . . . the Society intact.'

'The greater good,' said someone.

'They'd try to stop us, anyway,' said a woman.

'Yes,' said Susan. 'Yes. I know. They can't, though, can they? We did it. We did it! And now the time's arrived. Today, here and now, we shall summon Death itself.'

A murmur of voices washed through the house. I stared over at Danny, still not daring to move.

What did she say? he mouthed.

'I don't know. I want to go,' I whispered, pointing at the door. Danny looked sceptical.

'Just wait,' he said. 'Can you see?'

Slowly, desperate not to make any noise, I shifted my body, turning to look back into the main room. I guessed the group was standing in a circle. From the kitchen, I could see two of them, one with her back to us, the other, a man, next to her, staring at something I couldn't see.

'The book!' said Susan, and I jumped back, kicking the wall by accident. Danny flinched at the noise, and for a moment I was sure they had heard me, were about to run in, to haul us up and take us to the police.

'One copy, and we *found* it, my friends,' she was saying. 'And we have claimed it, and studied, and translated it, and now it is time. This is the place. Is everyone ready?'

'For our loved ones,' said one of the men. 'For our losses.'

'Yes,' said Susan, her voice quieter again. 'Yes. Cully, draw the circle, just as we practised. The inscription must be exact. I shall recite as you do so, and then, as agreed, we shall each submit the offering, and intone together. The power will be drawn in to the centre, and I will complete the binding. This is history, friends.'

'For Andrea, who should never have been taken,' said someone. They cleared their throat. 'We're with you, Susan. For the greater good.'

'Are they ... ?' said Danny, and he looked out from behind the counter. Susan was talking now, chanting something I couldn't understand, strange words that hissed and spat. One of the men – crouched down, chalk in his hand – was

45

moving around the room, his tongue stuck out in concentration, but then he was gone again, and I couldn't see what he was doing.

'This is bad,' said Danny. 'Phil, we have to—'

'What are they doing?' I muttered.

'Phil, come on, we can break this door.'

'Hang on, just let me see . . . '

Susan's words had changed now. They flew from her mouth, fluid and thick, pouring into the silence of the room, echoing through the air. The others were humming, quiet and loud, quiet and loud, a heartbeat, a wave of sound, and I felt the hairs on my arms begin to prickle.

'Offerings from your masters!' said someone, and I heard gasps, the hiss of sudden pain, heard the slice of knives against each other. I was creeping forward now, moving towards the doorway, desperate to see what was happening.

'Phil, *please*,' said Danny from behind me. The air felt thick, filled with static, crackling and smoking. I smelled lightning and blood and earth. Susan's voice was a roar now, and the line of chalk spat sparks and smoke, the people standing along it gripping each other's hands, their faces twisted in pain, blood trickling between their fingers. Only one woman stood apart, her face white, her eyes wide open and staring at nothing. Her hands were clasped around a dark green book, its yellowed pages glowing with flames and light.

'What the *hell*?'

46

Danny was beside me, staring at the group, jumping as the sparks filled the air, as an arch of brilliant lightning hissed through the air and split open one of the floorboards.

'We have to run!' he shouted at me, but it was too noisy now, and wind was ripping through the house, churning up dust and sand.

'Danny!' I shouted, and he grabbed my shoulders, pulling me back towards the kitchen door.

'Come on!' he said.

'OK! OK! I'm—'

With a sound like the roar of waves, a pulse of light, too bright to bear, shot from the centre of the group, rippled outwards, flooding the kitchen, washing over us, and then fell back in on itself, racing back towards the chalk circle. I heard screams, and the sound of breaking wood, and then I was falling, or maybe flying, and everything turned black.

'Bloody hell, you're heavy.'

Someone was pulling my arms. Something was tickling my neck. I opened my eyes and gasped, a jolt of pain in my chest.

'Oh, thank God,' said Danny. 'I thought – I mean, I didn't know if . . . '

It was dark, and beyond the roll of clouds I could see stars dotting the sky. My back was wet, my skin cold and clammy. I groaned.

'Um, what . . . ?'

'Phil, we have to move. They're still looking for us. They'll look here soon, I bet.'

'What? Where are we?'

Danny was crouched over me. His hands were shaking, his face shining with sweat.

'I dragged you here. It's a bunch of long grass further down the cliff. I figured we could hide for a bit.'

'You dragged me?'

'Yeah, look,' he said, pointing behind me. I sat up, my head aching, and peered through the thin light. Above us, up a steep bank, the silhouette of the house rose up against the sky.

'You kicked down the back door?'

'Yeah. You remember?'

'Yeah. I think. There was screaming, and that light, and—'

'Those people. We have to get out of here, Phil; they're still up there. They saw us!'

'But what were they *doing*?'

'*Really* more important things to focus on,' said Danny, and he grabbed my wrist, pulling me up.

'There was some sort of explosion,' he whispered. 'I don't think they're all OK. I couldn't carry you all the way back, but now you're up, we can run, try to get home.'

I rubbed my head, my ears ringing. 'They're still up there? What time is it?'

He pulled out his phone. The screen lit up his face. 'Almost seven.'

'Crap. What do we do?'

'We have to scramble up here, then round the house.'

I took a couple of deep breaths. My side ached. 'Did you drop me?' I asked.

Danny looked sheepish. 'You kind of . . . rolled a bit. Look, I had to do it—'

'It's fine,' I said. 'Thanks.'

'Cool. Ready?'

I turned to look behind us, away from the cliff, out to the ocean lost in the blackness. I could hear the waves now, see flashes and ripples of water if I squinted. I looked up at the stars and the cloud-licked moon.

'I'm freezing my nuts off,' said Danny. 'So . . . '

'Fine,' I said. 'After you.'

He pulled a face. 'You're sure you can climb this? I could go after you and—'

'And what, shove me? As if. Come on.'

For a moment I thought he might argue, but then he sniffed, rubbed his hands together, and started climbing up the bank. I watched as he got to the top, ducking down and slowly peeking over. He turned back to me.

'Coast's clear. Come on!'

'Hah,' I said quietly. 'Coast. Good. Yes. OK.'

I ran forward, using my hands to pull myself up, feeling the damp grass, the rough, sandy soil with my fingers. My

49

shoes slipped as I scrambled, but soon I was at the top, following Danny as he ducked low around the house, moving slowly, my breath fogging the night.

'They're here somewhere!' shouted a woman.

'You're *sure?*' said a man. George, I thought. His name was George.

'Oh, they're here,' said someone else – the man called Cully. 'I saw them too. Couple of brats. No idea what they've done!'

'Is Susan . . . ?'

'Susan will recover. But the damage – and what if they *talk?*'

'They won't. They *can't*. What would people say? And the Society!'

Patty, her name was. I remembered that. The voices were close. But where were they? We were running through the dark, around the house, and Danny wasn't slowing down. Hadn't he heard them? I ran faster, catching him up just as he came level with the front of the house.

'They're on the porch!' he whispered. 'There's no way to get down the drive without them seeing us!'

'Well, there's no way back,' I said. 'Unless you fancy a swim?'

He didn't reply. I could see him shifting his weight from foot to foot, clenching his hands.

'Got to leg it,' he said. 'They'll never catch us, not if we just keep going. Through the fence and all the way home.'

'They'll follow us!'

'Then ... then we go down into Metchley Road, and stop by the post office. If no one's followed us by that point, we know we're safe. Yeah?'

'I guess,' I whispered. 'But—'

'Good. On three, yeah?'

'This is mad,' I said. 'This is just mad.'

There was a burst of laughter on the porch, and then raised voices, an argument starting.

'One,' said Danny. He bent down, resting his fingertips of the ground.

'Two.' I swallowed. They were going to catch us. They were adults. What would they do?

'Three,' he said, and without another word, side by side, we started to run.

FOUR

'THERE! LOOK, there!'

They were shouting, screaming behind us, and I heard feet stomping on gravel, sliding on the grit and the sand, and we raced away from the house.

'Don't stop!' shouted Danny. 'Don't look back!'

The air was freezing but I gulped it in, pushing forward, my side aching, my hands numb from the cold. Danny was in front of me, a blur in the darkness, and the wind screeched in my ears. We kept going dead straight, the shouts from behind us getting quieter, and I heard panting and groaning. *They're out of shape*, I thought. *Good.*

A metallic rattle told me Danny had got to the fence, and soon he was pushing through it, looking back, reaching out his hand.

'Come on, come on!'

'I'm fine!' I said.

'Think they're following?'

'Yes!'

I squeezed between the metal posts, the chains that held them shut ringing like bells in the night. There was someone coming, one of the men, and as I pushed through I turned back, peering through the dark, searching for his face. I saw him, panting, his face shining, coming towards the fence, and for a moment our eyes met. He gave a roar and sped up, and Danny pulled at my shoulder.

'Run!' he shouted, and we set off again, down the road, back among houses, away from the biting wind of the coast. We ducked through parked cars and jumped walls, barely talking, panting and hurting and scared. My lungs burned, my whole body shaking with effort, and as we reached a corner, I called out.

'Just – wait, please. I have to rest.'

Danny came back, bending over, hands on his knees, gasping for breath.

'You'd be a rubbish rugby player,' he said.

'I'm OK with that.'

'I don't see anyone,' he said, straightening up.

'They can't have followed us.'

'Yeah?'

'There's no way. We'd have seen them. Anyway, they were slow, and they said some of them were hurt.'

'This is mental,' said Danny, rubbing his face, pacing back and forth. 'Properly mental. Did you see that *light*? And what were they *doing*? Was that ... was that magic?'

I shut my eyes, remembered the smell of fire and blood and lightning. 'No way,' I said. 'That's not real. Just a trick.'

'Damn good trick.'

'Yeah.'

I could hear my heartbeat pounding in my head. I tried to calm down, to make things seem right and normal again.

'I have to go home,' I said.

'Yeah. Yeah. They can't chase us now, eh?'

I brushed sand from my trousers, from the thick fabric of my school blazer.

'No,' I said. I wiped my eyes, stinging from the cold, from the salt, from the fear. 'No. We're good. We're safe. Right?'

'Yeah. Yeah. But, Phil—'

'I don't know,' I said. 'I don't know that that was. I don't know.'

'I don't . . . ' he said, but his voice was small, his face pale. We looked at each other, looked away.

'Come on,' I said. 'Home's this way.'

Neither of us saw the shapes moving in the shadows, heard the whispers that trickled down the road, smelled the smoke and the fire that flashed in the dark.

'I thought Mum was going to go spare. You're lucky they like you so much.'

'Gee, thanks.'

'And it helps that they're gullible. You *obviously* weren't at the shops. You're covered in sand!'

'Leave it, Jess.'

'Yeah, right.' She shifted closer to me, pushing a pile of clothes onto the floor.

'Your room's a mess,' she said.

'Jess, please, I just want to go to bed.'

For a second she looked like she was going to complain, but then she huffed, jumped off the bed and moved towards the door.

'Fine, whatever. Just be careful, yeah?'

'I'm fine,' I said. 'It's all fine.'

Maybe it showed on my face, because Jess stopped, hand on the door, and her voice changed a bit, became serious, almost a whisper.

'No one's giving you trouble, right?'

I smiled and tried to look relaxed. 'I appreciate you going into big sister mode,' I said. 'If I need your help in a rumble, I'll let you know.'

'Sock 'em with my sick moves,' she said.

'Now you're just quoting song lyrics. I'm fine! Really.'

'Mysterious weirdo,' said Jess, but then she chuckled, walking out and shutting the door behind her.

I waited for a couple of minutes, listening to the sounds of the house, the buzz of the TV downstairs, Jess turning the taps on in the bathroom, humming to herself. I pulled my phone out and messaged Danny: *Home safe? Parents mad?*

Almost as soon as the message had sent, my phone chirruped, and Danny's name came up.

Yeah. All fine here, Soz, shoulda said.

'Well, thanks for that,' I muttered.

Definitely no one followed? I said. I walked to the window, pulling back the curtain and looking out at the road.

Don't think so, said Danny. Then, before I could reply, *But . . . maybe boy outside earlier? Thought I saw.*

I frowned, looking back at the road, up and down in the dark, and then stepped away from the window to type my reply.

Someone here?

A few minutes went by before he answered. I thought about calling him, or running next door to ask him what he meant, but I knew I was being silly. Still, those people, and that light, and those words . . .

Forget it, said Danny. *Nothing. Just mad. C u at school. Gnite.*

'Well, what the hell does that mean?' I said.

Sure? I typed. The message sent, but this time Danny wasn't replying. Minutes ticked past. Jess was talking to Mum and Dad downstairs, and then laughing about something, and there was music on the TV. A siren was moving down a street nearby, its tone shifting and fading. I felt annoyed suddenly, that things didn't make sense, that after the rush and the fear there was . . . just this. Nothing. Sitting in my room, listening to a sleepy town. I threw my phone down on the bed, staring at my wall, imagining Danny in the house next door, not even bothering to see if I'd asked anything else. I went back to the window, tugged the curtains open, saw my reflection, the blackness in the glass, and then . . . I jumped backwards, knocking a glass of water off my desk. I knelt down, grabbing the glass, ignoring the water as it seeped into the carpet. My heart was racing, a sudden burst of panic and fear. Slowly, peering through the bottom corner of the window, I looked out again. A girl, no older than me, her thin hair moving in the wind, was standing on the pavement across from the house. She stared up at me, her face impossible to read – confused? surprised? – and then she smiled, raising one hand to wave. I ducked below the window again, my mind buzzing. A girl from school? I was sure I'd never seen her before. And why would anyone be here? No, she wasn't a friend. One of Jess's friends, then? I crouched down and headed for the hallway, looking back to make sure the curtains were closed. Something about that girl gave me the creeps. At the top of the stairs I called down.

'Hey, Jess?'

A pause, then the rustle of the sofa cushions, and the living-room door opened, light spilling into the hallway.

'Yeah?'

'You have a friend coming round?'

She looked at her watch. 'What? No. Why?'

'It's too late for friends, Philippa!' called Dad.

'You invited someone round?' she asked, sounding almost impressed.

'No, no, I just … thought I saw someone, thought they might be for you.'

'Really?'

She moved to the front door, pulling it open before I could call out.

'Wait, no!'

She looked annoyed now. 'Is this some dumb game? Philippa, seriously, I don't—'

I ignored her, running down the stairs to look out into the road. The pavement was empty, the cold air biting at my face.

'You're letting the heat out!' Dad shouted.

'Philippa's gone mad!' said Jess.

'Oh, there's news,' he laughed.

'I guess … sorry. I guess it was just someone passing.'

'Think you're the centre of attention, eh? Not everyone who walks past is hoping for an audience.'

'Ha bloody ha,' I said, and I shut the front door, making sure the chain was on.

At breakfast the next day Mum looked annoyed and shook her head.

'Under the weather?' she said. 'That's what you get for staying out in the cold, hmm?'

'Mum,' I said. She tutted and passed me some toast.

'Eat up,' she said. I wasn't hungry but I took a few bites.

I looked out of the window, at the garden and the morning mist, and felt nervous. I looked at my phone. No messages. No calls.

'Morning!' said my sister. She was already dressed and ready to go. She smiled at me and flicked on the kettle.

'Sleep well?'

'Sure,' I said, barely raising my head.

She looked at my mum, pulling a face. 'Young people today, eh?'

'I don't know where they get it from.'

'I blame the home life,' I said, and Mum tapped the back of my head in answer.

Upstairs, in the bathroom, I saw the girl again. I was doing my hair, lost in thought, when my eyes slipped to the window, and the garden beneath it, and the girl who was standing there, watching me, frowning. I swore, jumped back, and knocked the mug of toothbrushes flying. It fell to the floor, smashing on the tiles, flecks of white and grey skidding around my feet.

'Crap, crap, crap!'

I looked up again. The garden was empty. I was breathing too fast. I had to calm down.

'Oi, everything all right?' called Jess.

'Yeah! Yeah. Dropped the mug. Broke it.'

'Oh, Philippa. Is my toothbrush on the floor? Ew.'

'Sorry. Sorry.'

'You owe me a new one.'

'We can afford to get you as many as you like,' Mum called. 'Now come on, sweetie. Time to get to school.'

I tried to think. I could say I was sick. I could try to stay at home. But then what? Hide-and-seek with a ghost-girl? I'd rather be with people. I'd rather know I wasn't going crazy.

'Yeah, sure. Coming.' I looked out into the garden again, but it was empty, the grass a pale, sickly green, and the sky was nothing but rainclouds. I blinked and swallowed, telling myself that I had imagined it, that it was a trick of the light, of mist, of reflections on glass.

I looked at my phone again. Nothing from Danny. That made me feel strange and I sent off another message: *Walk to school together?*

Five minutes later, walking out the door, he hadn't replied. The curtains to his bedroom were still drawn shut.

The day passed slowly. Around me the school buzzed and moved and trudged along. My mind wandered in lessons, my feet dragged as I walked through the hallway. I looked around for Danny but I couldn't find him, and his phone rang and rang without an answer. Was he sick? Or something worse? I tried to remember the names of the men and women in the house. They wouldn't come here, though, would they?

If this was a movie, and I was some hardened New Yorker, I knew exactly what I'd say right now. *God, I need a drink.* But I wasn't. I was a kid in school, and I suddenly felt very alone. It was English class, right before lunch. I sat in the back, my usual spot, and listened to the others take it in turns to read *Lord of the Flies.* Miss Flynn was at her desk, following along, smiling at us, helping the ones who tripped over their words. I tried to focus. Who was reading? Marcus LeNeve. His voice was flat and confused.

'"The fair boy shook his head."' Marcus read. '"This is an island. At least I think it's an island. That's a reef out in the sea. Perhaps there aren't any grown ups anywhere."'

I shivered and tried not to think about last night. Rose Primer looked over at me, rolled her eyes, made a big yawn gesture. I smiled and nodded, though I quite liked the book. She leaned backwards in her chair, and I saw through the window, in the playground outside, the girl from this morning, standing, smiling, and watching me.

I didn't jump. I didn't fall out of my chair. I stared at her, this girl I didn't know, and I tried to be sensible. I was in school, surrounded by people. She wasn't even in uniform. She wasn't allowed to be here. I didn't take my eyes off her, and her strange smile, and the way the wind didn't move her hair, and I raised my hand.

'Miss?'

'Yes, Philippa?'

'Miss, there's a girl out there not from our school.'

'Hmm?' She sounded confused, maybe bored. I pointed out of the window. Heads turned. Kids on the other side got out of their seats to look, to have something to do.

'Sit down, guys!' called Miss Flynn. 'Philippa, what are you saying?'

'There, out the window, that girl. She shouldn't be here, should she?'

She tilted her head to look of out the classroom window, scanning up and down, and the girl shook her head, slowly, like I'd made a joke.

'What girl?' said Miss Flynn. Rose Primer was frowning, trying to follow where I pointed.

'Where is she?'

'She's there! Right there!' I said. Rose pulled a face. Miss Flynn sniffed.

'No time for distractions,' she said. 'Marcus, you were reading. Keep going, now!'

'But, Miss!' I said.

'Philippa, please.'

'She's right there!'

They were sniggering now, whispering to each other. Miss Flynn sighed and stood up. She walked up next to me and looked out of the window. The girl had started waving, wiggling her fingers, not moving from where she was stood.

'There's no reason to worry,' said Miss Flynn, her voice gentle, like she was talking to a spooked horse. 'There's no one here who shouldn't be. OK?'

I looked at her, at the girl through the window, and I started to feel afraid.

'Y-yeah. Of course. Sorry.'

'Maybe it was a ghost!' said someone. Others joined in, laughing, calling out. Darren O'Reily stood up, raised his hands like he was casting a spell. 'Ooooooooh!' he wailed.

'All right, enough! Back to *Lord of the Flies*, if you please!'

Everyone settled down, still whispering, still looking at me. Rose leaned over.

'Nice try,' she said, flicking her head towards Marcus as he began his monotonous reading.

'But I didn't—'

I felt hot and cold and weary.

'Yeah,' I said. 'Sure.'

When I looked back out at the girl she was gone.

Lunchtime came and I ran to the dining room, to the crowds and the noise and the smell of salt and chips. Danny's phone rang too long. Why wasn't he answering? This wasn't right.

Please call me, I texted. *Something bad happening.*

My lunch sat in front of me, uninspiring, smelling of grease. I played with the chips, ripped open packets of ketchup.

'You look grim!' said Jess, sitting down next to me and sliding her tray next to mine.

'Just tired.'

'Uh huh. What's up?'

'Nothing, Jess.'

'Philippa, come on.'

'Nothing's up! Just ... I just feel a bit strange. That's all.'

She laughed and stole one of my chips. 'What's new?'

My phone was in my hand. I looked at it, put it down, picked it up again.

'Won't call you back, huh? You guys had a fight?'

'What?'

'Danny,' she said. 'Come on. You're not exactly subtle. What's going on with you two?'

'It's not that. Really.' Jess raised an eyebrow.

'Well, if there is anything ... '

'Thanks.'

I looked out of the window. Kids were playing. The sun had come out. I scanned their faces, peered into the shadows, tried to find her.

'Lost someone?'

'There's a new girl,' I said. 'I've seen her a couple of times. I just want to ... make sure she's OK.'

'That's very generous of you.'

She knew I was lying. I didn't care. We ate in silence, Jess looking up, watching people, me looking at my phone, writing messages to Danny, deleting them, saving drafts.

'Well, this has been a hoot,' said Jess, 'but I'm going to be off. You sure you're—'

'Yes! Go. Really. Just tired, like I said. Out late. Didn't sleep.'

'OK, weirdo.'

She grabbed her bag, picked up her tray, and headed off into the crowd. I wished she hadn't left. I suddenly felt alone.

I was halfway home when my phone finally buzzed. I felt it in my pocket and my hand flew for it before it had even stopped.

1 New Message, said the screen. I flicked my thumb across the glass and pulled up my messages. Danny! He wasn't dead or lost or mad! I smiled, then felt stupid, and clicked the button to read it.

Hey, wrote Danny, *sorry for not replying. Weird day. Too weird. Phone wasn't on and I didn't notice. Phil, can you come here as soon as poss? Gotta talk. Majorly messed up. You met yours yet? She might be shy. Mine's here. Can't believe all this. Lemme know you get this k?*

'What the hell?' I whispered. I read the message twice, then three times, then again. Messed up? Met mine? I frowned, pulled my hair back behind my ear and tried to ignore the growing feeling of panic. *She might be shy. She.* The girl? But how would Danny know about her if he hadn't been at school? I looked up from my phone again and checked the street. It was empty, a grey river of concrete and houses. A lick of wind rustled the bare leaves on a too-thin tree. Could I hear the waves from here? I tried, but there was too much distraction, too much clatter from the town. It was amazing how quickly it got lost, that mighty ocean, as soon as you turned your back on it. I sighed, started walking again – I was only ten minutes from home by now – and texted back.

What does any of that mean? Who's she? I'll be there soon. I'll knock. You OK?

The message sent and I gripped my phone tight, walking faster than before. A cat crossed the road in front of me, shining white with black paws, a streak of lightning through the houses. It stopped, turned its head to see me, and changed course, pleased to have someone to boss around.

'Hey,' I said. 'I can't stop . . . '

It rubbed against my legs, twisting around and circling like something ancient and slippery. I bent down – the cat backed away, then melted back towards me – and I scratched its head, rubbing along its back. It purred and pushed back. I liked cats. They were confident in everything.

'His name is Calum,' said the girl. She was standing right in front of me, so close I could have touched her, looking down at me and the cat. She looked nervous, hesitant, like she might fly away. I thought of a flock of birds, ready to scatter in a thousand directions. The cat arched its back and hissed, bolting away from the girl. She raised her hand, flexed her fingers, and the cat froze, cocked its head, and trotted back. It sat in front of her, tail swishing the road, and looked up, perfectly still.

'Calum is the name his family gave him, anyway. I am sure he has others.'

She hadn't been there a second ago. She hadn't, had she? Where had she come from? I would have seen her. It wasn't possible.

'Who are you?' I said. I wanted to sound angry and powerful. My voice squeaked and I took a step back. 'You were outside my house – and then at school! You're following me!'

'I did not want to scare you. I did not know how to ... how to say hello.'

'Well, who are you, then?'

She looked down at the cat and bit her lip. 'Shoo,' she said, and without another sound the cat slipped away across the road, under a bush, out of sight.

'It is complicated. Let's go to Danny's. He can help. He gets it.'

'You know Danny? Hold on—'

She was already moving down the road. Anger burst open in me. 'Hey! You can't just— I mean it, who are you? What's your name?'

She stopped and turned back to look at me. Her hair was dark – not black, I saw, when it moved in the light, but thick and long, well past her shoulders. Her eyes were a strange light green. She was small, too – not young, really, just ... somehow off, like she was delicate, more ghost than girl. She met my eyes and nodded.

'You're right. Sorry. My name is ... Dee.'

'Just Dee?'

'Just Dee. I am a friend, Philippa. Your friend. Really.'

'Sure. And you just followed me to school?'

She smiled again, but there was something there – was she laughing? Tired?

'I was not sure how to approach you,' she said. 'But now we have ... what could you say? Broken the ice, I suppose ...'

She trailed off, the words hanging dead in the air.

'You're friends with them,' I said, 'aren't you? That group we saw, the ones who—'

'I am not. Believe me, I am not. If we go to Danny's, it will be easier to explain.'

'No way! And if you think—'

My phone buzzed again. I glanced at it, taking another step away from Dee.

Hurry up then, said Danny. *Just come OK? If the girl is with you bring her too.*

That stumped me. He knew about her? What had he been up to today? I looked at her again, at her face, the way she held back, and I sighed.

'Fine,' I said. 'I'm heading to Danny's. You can come if you want, but ... just stay where I can see you, yeah?'

A seagull was flying overhead. Its screech was harsh and almost lonely.

'I know the way,' said Dee.

'Yeah, from stalking my house!'

'I did not ... stalk. I was just watching you. You will understand.'

'You're weird,' I said, and we starting walking again. For a few minutes we moved in silence, Dee's eyes fixed straight ahead or on the road. She looked at the world from behind a blank face, but something about her eyes made me think she was much, much younger than she looked. A dog barked behind a fence and she stopped to stare at the wooden panels.

'Come on,' I said. 'That's just Biscuit. He's safe.'

'Biscuit the dog,' she said.

'You're *so* weird. How do you know Danny?'

She looked surprised. 'I do not. This will be our first meeting.'

'What? Then how does he know you're with me?'

She shrugged, her hair bouncing down her back. I grunted and pulled my backpack tighter.

'Fine. Almost there, but I guess you knew that, eh?'

'Danny lives next to you. Yes.'

That look again, a smile, a flash of fear. I couldn't get a read on this girl.

'Right. Yeah.'

We rounded the corner. I could already see Danny standing outside his house, leaning against the wall and waiting for me. He was alone, and when he saw me, he waved, and called out like an impatient kid, 'Come on! Come on, Phil!'

'Why is he so—' I started saying, but I looked at Dee and stopped.

'He is excited.'

'Well done, genius.'

I sped up, and now Dee trailed behind me as I walked up to Danny and gave him a questioning look. 'Dude, what have you been doing? Did you stay home sick?'

He didn't answer. He coughed, pushed himself up off the wall, straightened his T-shirt. He was looking at Dee, his mouth open, like he was amazed and afraid all at once.

'Oi!' I said, punching his arm.

'Ow! No, I'm not sick. But look, Phil. Look at her! Did she tell you what she is? How are you so calm?'

'I'm so pissed, is what I am. What do you mean, what she is? I only just met her!'

'You – what? Like, just now?'

'I am not quite as ... direct as Garth,' said Dee, and she looked up at Danny's window.

'I swear, guys, you're all being so—'

'Phil,' said Danny, his voice low and serious and not like him at all, 'you don't understand—'

'I know I don't!'

'No! Listen! Keep quiet, OK? Phil, you have to listen to this. Dee – she isn't human!'

FIVE

W E WALKED up the stairs to Danny's room without saying anything. He led the way, looking back at me, electrified, excited. Dee was behind me, moving without seeming to make any sound at all.

'Here, in here,' said Danny.

'I know which one your room is,' I said. I'd been here hundreds of times. What was different?

Danny pushed his door open and nodded towards his bed.

'It's not the room I want to show you,' he said. A boy was sitting on the bed, cross-legged, a thin smile growing into a grin. His feet were bare, his hair shaved so short he was almost bald. His eyes were so blue they seemed to glow, his dark skin impossibly smooth. He smiled, his teeth a flash of white, and I thought of the Cheshire cat, and his grin, and his madness.

'Dee!' he said, springing up.

'Garth, I told you I would be back. It's been one day.'

71

The boy shrugged. 'I'm new to this. It's weird being . . . separate.'

He turned to me and Danny. His eyes were more violet than blue, I realised, but they were still unnaturally bright.

'Philippa,' he said. 'Yes, I recognise you.'

'Um, have we . . . met?'

'Yesterday I saw you in the house by the water,' said the boy, 'though you wouldn't have seen me, no. Danny, should I . . . ?'

Danny stepped towards the boy, standing next to him, their shoulders almost touching. They were smiling like wolves.

'This is Garth,' said Danny. 'This is why I skipped school today. And you know Dee' – he gestured towards her – 'though I guess you didn't have as much time together yet. Look, Phil, there's no easy way to explain this – I'm going to try – but these two, they're not . . . like us.'

'Not human, you said.'

He rubbed the back of his neck. 'Yeah. Yeah, they're not.'

'Then what are they?'

'It's kind of . . . ' He trailed off.

Dee spoke up. 'Yesterday, a group of people carried out an . . . experiment. Or, they tried to. The group – they call themselves the Society – were the ones you saw. They are not good people. They are trying to control something they have no right to. They don't know what they are doing. They are trying to get power, but magic is precise and you need

72

the right environment. You have to know so many things. In the house, they thought they were alone, but they were not. You and Danny were there. They had not counted on your presence, and so their . . . their magic, what they were trying to do, it went . . . wrong.'

'Did you just say *magic*?'

Danny let out a single bark of laughter. He was hyper, a kid with too much candy. He couldn't be serious. I looked at this girl, Dee, with her strange eyes, her strange face.

'What've you been telling him?' I said.

'Only the truth. The spell went wrong because of you.'

'Wait, we didn't do anything! And those people were—'

'It's OK. You didn't do anything wrong,' said Dee. 'But you being there added an unexpected element. Their calculations were off.'

'What is this experiment, exactly?' This felt wrong, like some huge trick, but why would Danny be so gullible, so childish? Everything felt off. I cleared my throat. 'What were they doing in that house?'

The boy, Garth, looked grim. 'It was a summoning. Bad magic. Not something they should be able to do. There are some forces, some things that should not be toyed with, cannot be made to sit and roll over like some puppy. The invocation is not meant to exist, but it does, and they found it, and they worked out how to use it. They are foolish children playing with dark fire.'

He crossed his arms, and for one second, it seemed like his

eyes were blazing, throwing light against the bedroom wall. I flinched, stepped back. These kids were mad – probably dangerous.

'Magic. Right. Sure. So—'

'Phil, just listen,' said Danny. I scowled at him.

'The ceremony had one purpose,' said Dee, 'and that was to summon a force, a – a being – that you know as Death.'

Danny sucked in his breath. I stifled a laugh. 'OK.'

'Obviously, it didn't work,' said Garth.

'Obviously.'

'It failed because of you two.'

'Oh, yeah. Heroes, we are.'

'Phil,' said Danny, a warning note in his voice.

'What?'

'I know how it sounds,' said Dee, 'but . . . it's true. '

'So who are you, then? Wizards? Goblins? Should I be watching out for faerie food?'

'The Society opened a door,' said Garth. 'They shouldn't have been able to, but they did. When the invocation went wrong, that door slammed shut – but something was already being dragged through. Imagine a gate snapping shut just as you've put your foot through the door.'

'Yeah?'

'Well, that's . . . us,' said Garth. 'Something came through, but before anything else could, the balance was lost, and things tumbled out of control. Dee and I, we're . . . spectres, you could say. We were left here, cut off and alone, suddenly, and we latched on to the nearest things we could.'

I knew the answer before I'd finished asking the question. 'And what was that?'

'Us!' said Danny.

I looked from face to face, trying to work out the joke, the game they were playing. Danny's room was a mess – it always was – and I took in the piles of clothes, the sports stuff, the books, the old games. Someone was playing music in a car outside. The bass thudded and bled through the windows.

'Dee and I are spirits of something much bigger than you can understand,' said Garth, 'but we're not your enemies. I am attached to Danny. Dee is attached to you. We were ripped away from our homes and orphaned here in a single moment, and we found shelter and form by connecting with you.'

'Garth is amazing, Phil!' said Danny. 'We spent the day – I woke up and he was here and, I mean, of course I was scared, but then he showed me, and I saw how real it all was, and . . . you have to see. You have to see what they can do!'

Drugs, maybe? Had they threatened him? I stepped backwards.

'What d'you mean?'

'We are cut off from our home,' said Dee, 'but that does not make us useless. Let us show you something. Will you agree? To open your mind and look?'

The music had stopped. Danny's curtains were half-closed, making the light grimy and thin as the sun slunk lower.

'This is ... a lot,' I said finally.

'I know, I know!' said Danny. 'But, Phil, this is ... I mean, this is big. Huge! Magic! And Death himself!'

'Herself,' said Dee.

'Himself,' said Garth. They looked at each other, raised their eyebrows, and laughed. Their eyes flashed with light.

'Garth was able to show me stuff,' said Danny, 'and Dee can do the same to you. OK? Give her your hand. That's all.'

'You sound like a cult,' I told him. He winked.

'Gift of the gab, me.'

Dee had sat down on the side of the bed.

'What do you want to show me?' I said.

'A place that's far away.'

'How, then?'

'Give me your hand, and I can.'

This didn't feel right. I was jumpy, nervous, ready to bolt – but Danny seemed so sure, so calm, and I trusted him ...

'This is mental,' I said. Danny just grinned. 'This is some stupid game, isn't it? If your rugby mates are—'

'Oh, let it go, Phil! You just have to see! You trust me, don't you? We're friends, right? Right?'

He was getting angry, frustrated, clutching at whatever would work. Dee and Garth watched us, their faces blank.

There was something *off* about the way they sat, the way they moved. It made me want to run. My hand was on the door.

'Danny—'

'Do this for me. For us. Yeah?'

He sounded so small now, so bloody young. I swallowed and looked at Dee.

'OK,' I said, 'I'm game. Show me this amazing thing.'

Danny let out a yelp of joy, rocking the bed as he moved. Garth smiled.

'It's safe,' said Dee.

'That doesn't make me feel better.'

'Oh, man, I'm so glad you're here, Phil,' said Danny. He stood up, moved close to me, squeezed my shoulder. 'Come sit here,' he said, guiding me, and then he was beside me, so close our legs were touching.

'All together, yeah?' he said. The others nodded, holding hands. Garth reached for Danny's, who reached for mine. My palms were sweaty and cold.

'Danny, what—' I began, but he cut me off.

'Stop asking questions, man! Come on, let her show you.'

Slowly, as if I might be electrocuted, I reached down and took Dee's hand. It was warmer than I'd expected, and soft – more like velvet than skin. I shivered.

'If this is some joke,' I said.

'Breathe,' said Dee. 'And I'll guide you.'

'Oh yeah, first star to the right and straight on till bloody morning,' I muttered.

'You don't know the half of it,' said Danny.

There was a flash of light, and the sound of far-away wind, and suddenly, impossibly, we were somewhere completely new.

The mountain was huge – impossibly huge – and it towered over a sky that shimmered and crackled with stars. They lay across the sky in lazy brushstrokes, bright against the darkness, cluttered, sparkling. It was the most beautiful thing I had ever seen. Beneath the stars the land spread out, a forest at night, warm, filled with pools of water and the sound of insects and birds and life. I gasped, fell backwards, felt hard rock press against my hands. We were standing on a path that wound around the mountain as far as I could see.

'Oh my God,' I said, and I felt my legs buckle. 'What ... ? How ... ?'

Danny was beside me, his hand on my shoulder, his voice calm and clear. 'Give it a sec. I did the same. I know. I know. But we're here. We really are.'

Wind was flowing up from the forest, and it smelled of grass and lavender. I felt Dee and Garth standing over me, looking down, looking up at the sky, looking down at me again.

'How did we—'

'That was me,' said Dee. 'I brought you here. I thought you would like to see it.'

'See *what*? What is this?'

She bit her lip. 'It's a ... between place.'

'It's hard to explain,' said Garth. 'This place isn't really a place, I mean. Not like you're thinking, like it's real rock, a real world.'

Danny put his hand on my shoulder. 'Don't worry, I don't get it either. But I think this is like a ... a train station between where we come from and ... other places.'

I tried to work out if he was joking, if he was mad. 'What?'

'Dee and I are not human,' said Garth. He kicked at a pebble on the path and it plummeted silently into the air below. 'We come from somewhere else – you might call it the spirit world. It lies beyond humanity. There are other places, Philippa. Other dreams and mirrors.'

'We're cut off from home,' said Dee. 'That Society made sure of that. We're stranded on the wrong side of the glass, and this is the closest we can get to home. An in-between place. A reflection. This is the World Between.'

'This makes no sense,' I said, and I was breathing too fast, hot and panicked.

'It freaked me out, too,' said Danny. 'I got Garth to bring me here and take me back, and bring me here again,' he said. 'And ... I mean, can't you feel it? This place is so alive. It's another world! A world between worlds!'

'It's not much,' said Garth, looking like he wanted to be humble. 'If you think of a train station, this is more like the sign pointing to the platforms. But . . . it is proof, isn't it?'

'Convinced me,' said Danny. He put his hands on the back of his neck, puffed out his chest, a great big grin on his face. 'Another world!' he shouted, and the sound echoed before dying out. 'The human world, the spirit world, and this place, the no man's land, but we get to see it, Phil. We get to *feel* it!'

'So you see?' said Dee. She touched my arm lightly, not in a mean way, and I opened my mouth to say something, closed it again, looked into her shining eyes.

'You're not human,' I said.

'No.'

'Then you're . . . what?'

'A long way from home. And we need your help.'

There was a silent, brilliant white flash of light, and I felt the ground warp and bubble beneath me. The rock shifted, my balance was thrown, and I threw my arms out as I fell. Carpet. The smell of old clothes. Danny's bedroom, the early evening sun dribbling in through his curtains.

'We're back,' said Garth.

'Oh, man!' said Danny. 'I wanted to explore!'

Garth's face turned more serious. 'You should be careful even there,' he said. 'It's not always a safe place. It's not meant for you.'

Someone was kneeling beside me. Dee had her hands in her lap and she spoke quietly, almost whispering.

'When we came through, when we were –' she paused, flinching '– cut off from home, we attached to you. Garth to Danny, me to you. Those others, they reeked of magic and greed. You two were children and you were scared, but you were good. We could tell. We're attached to you. Please. We need your help.'

'Why do you need my help?'

She stood up again, moving sideways to stand next to Garth. They looked solemn and scared, but angry, almost defiant.

'We need to go home,' said Garth, 'and for that, we need the book.'

They were looking at me, the three of them, and I felt a stab of annoyance that Danny knew so much more than me.

'How come you were together all day,' I said, 'but Dee and me only just met?'

'We're not the same person,' said Dee. 'Garth was more confident in his approach. I thought caution might be best.'

'You made everyone at school think I'm a nutter!'

'We also had to be wary, then. This is untested water.'

'It's never happened before,' said Garth. 'Being cut off from home? Being by ourselves, away from ... from everything else? No. There's no rule book.'

'Everything else,' I muttered.

'Phil,' said Danny, using his best *play nice* voice. 'How can

81

we say no? Have you ever heard anything like this? I mean, they're . . . they're basically angels, right?'

'Or demons.'

'Or just friends,' said Garth.

'So what's this book?'

Garth pulled a face. 'Humans are always trying to mess with spirits. Magic and summoning and invocations. It's a waste of time. Making contact with the other side is almost impossible.'

'Almost?'

He grimaced. 'There is a book. It's old, you know. I don't even know how old.' He looked at Dee. 'It's weird, this. Having thoughts. Having my . . . my own memories.'

'You don't have them over on –' Danny faltered '– where you're from?'

Dee's face darkened. 'We're not *us* there. We're not meant to be. It's all one, one great big force, perfect and pure and good and never-ending. Garth and me, we were made the second we were stranded here. We had to have form, have our own life. It's wrong. It shouldn't happen. Death is absolute. We shouldn't be . . . shattered.'

'You talk about Death like it's this great thing,' said Danny.

'I talk about it because I know it,' said Dee. 'It's not good or bad. It just is. We just were. Are. Oh, this is impossible . . . !'

She was tripping over her words, flustered by trying to say something she couldn't. I felt sorry for her.

'The book,' I said. 'Tell me about it.'

Garth was staring at an empty spot of air, his eyes losing some of their brightness. 'Yes,' he said. 'I remember. The book. There was a man – he was a witch doctor, I suppose. He worked hard to contact spirits, control them, to learn forbidden things. He was special and he was lucky. He was good at what he did, and he had power – real power – that I've never seen in any other priest or shaman or witch. He was a true sorcerer, but then he ... well, he died.'

'Told you school was dangerous,' muttered Danny.

I shoved him. 'Keep going,' I said.

'He was sick. He had a fever, a terrible thing. He died, and so we came to him, Death in all our power, and he was different – unafraid, cocky, with his questions.'

He looked up at us again. 'People are normally scared. They're shaken and confused and lots try to run away or bargain or play games. He was different. He thought he already understood us. He didn't argue or shout. He just –' he frowned, like he was remembering a half-forgotten story '– he asked us things. Questions we'd never been asked before, but he asked them, and he was dead, so we ... we answered him.'

When I spoke, my voice was barely a whisper. 'You spoke to his soul. So souls exist? This is ... this is amazing! Danny, do you know what—'

'Shh,' he said. He was watching Garth. The spectre stared back.

'But then something happened. He was pulled back to the living world, his heart beating with blood, his brain crackling with sparks and hope. He lived. He survived.'

'Resuscitated,' said Dee. 'Chance. You call it fluke?' She looked like she was tasting the word for the first time. 'He got away.'

'Magic?' said Danny, before I had a chance to ask it myself. Dee shook her head.

'Just plain medicine. Nothing special. He just . . . how would you say? Didn't go into the light.' She smiled. 'But he remembered. I don't think others would have, or they would have called it a dream, or a vision, or madness. Not him. He remembered the secrets he had learnt. And there he was, a living man, and he *knew* things, things no one can know. What does someone do with something like that?'

I knew the answer. 'He wrote them down.'

'We learnt our lesson then,' said Garth. 'We don't share secrets now. We don't answer questions. Not until it's too late to turn back. No more chances. No more clever people bargaining and boasting.' He raised his voice. 'We are Death and we are absolute.'

Danny looked at me. My stomach felt cold with something like fear.

'That book,' said Dee, 'has passed from hand to hand, all these years, and no one has been stupid enough, or brilliant enough, to think to use it. Until . . . '

'That bunch of idiots?' said Danny, and he sounded like he might laugh. 'You're saying *they* are the only ones to ... to call you? To call Death?'

'They are dangerous,' said Dee. Her eyes were fire, dancing with light. Her fingers flexed and light shone in their tips.

'But they sounded so *normal*,' said Danny. 'I mean, they could have been our parents' friends.'

'They're not your friends,' said Dee.

'No, I know. I just meant—'

'So you're saying those people tried ... magic?' I said. It made me feel weird, thinking of the house, how we were there only yesterday, and how far away it felt.

'They were children toying with a monster,' said Garth. 'But ... yes, magic, if you want. They almost succeeded. It was you two who stopped them, really. Too many people, it threw off the balance. And ... '

He made a slicing motion with his hand. 'Snip!' Danny winced.

'We just want to go home,' said Dee. 'But we need the book. It really is the only way to open up a bridge. I mean, that or—'

She stopped, looking at Garth. He shook his head. She sighed.

'Wait, what?' I said, but at that moment I heard feet on the stairs, and a woman's voice called out from just below.

'Danny, love! I'm home!'

'Your mum!' I hissed. 'Guys, you have to hide!'

'Phil, wait, you have to see this,' said Danny. 'Just chill, OK? Just watch.'

He looked proud of himself, his grin returning. He sat down on his bed like a satisfied cat. I made a mental note to punch him sometime soon.

'But—'

'You'll see.'

I sighed and turned to the door, glancing again at Garth and Dee, at their strange eyes, their blank faces, wondering how Danny was going to explain this. The footsteps had reached the landing now, and then a hand pushed open Danny's door, and his mum was there, smiling when she saw me.

'Oh, Philippa! I didn't know you were here. Are you staying for tea?'

I looked at her, at Garth and Danny, back at her. 'Um. Uh, no. No, thank you.'

She nodded and turned to Danny, her eyes passing over the others. 'Danny, really, this bedroom is a mess! I take it you're feeling better if you're having company.'

'Mum, Phil isn't *company*.'

'She's alive with a sense of smell. Clean your room, eh, love?'

'Mum!'

This was too weird, but I forced myself to act normal, to rise to the bait. 'Oh, is she embarrassing you, Danny?'

His smile flickered, but he shook his head and shrugged. 'As if,' he said. Then, 'I will, Mum. Promise.'

'OK, then. Nice to see you, Philippa.'

'You too, Mrs Perkins.'

'Take care, kids.'

She left, pulling the door closed after her. I let out a shuddering laugh.

'You're *invisible*?'

'Well, not to you,' said Garth.

I looked at Dee. 'That's why no one could see you at school!'

She nodded, her eyes brighter than ever. 'Not of this world,' she said. 'Not part of it, not seen by it.'

'We're the only ones who can see them!' said Danny. He jumped up off the bed, a kid at Christmas who got to unwrap his present early. 'Like, no one else in the world! They can't even pick things up, Phil!'

'Don't be too happy about it . . .' muttered Garth.

'You're just ghosts,' I said, looking at Dee. She blinked.

'Sure. If you want. But we need your help.'

'And you'll have it!' said Danny. 'Defeat the cult, get the book, save the world, and get owed one by Death himself! Not a bad day's work, eh, Philly?'

He plopped down on the bed again, crossing his legs and looking up at me expectantly. Seconds went past, one, two, three, and I stared at them, opening and closing my mouth like a dying fish. What could I do? How could I say no? I thought about the house, the crashing waves, the way those people had spoken . . .

'Don't call me Philly,' I said. 'And I'm not doing any crime fighting with you until you shave, you moron.'

SIX

'ARE YOU OK, love?'

I jabbed a carrot with my fork, bit down on it slowly.

'Hmm?'

'I said, are you OK? You're miles away!'

'Hmm?'

'Philippa, don't ignore your mother, please,' said Dad. I snapped back, saw them all looking at me.

'What? Sorry. Yeah, I'm fine.'

Dee was standing in the kitchen, watching my family with interest. I tried not to look at her, and ended up looking at her more. Jess gave me a quizzical look and turned her head to follow my gaze. Dee looked back, smiling. She winked.

'She's high,' said Jess. 'Only answer. Scourge of our society, you know. So sad.'

'Thank you, Jess,' said Dad.

'Don't worry, I'm far more into drink than drugs,' I said. 'I've seen what they did to poor Jess, and I swore off for life.'

'I am blessed,' said Mum, 'to have such open and honest children. But you're sure you're all right?'

'I'm fine,' I said, looking down again, catching an errant pea as it rolled across the table.

'They can't see me,' said Dee. 'There is no way. We're part of two different worlds. Don't worry.'

'I'm not worried,' I said.

'Who said you are?' said Dad.

'What? Oh, no, no one, I was just still joking. You know. Drugs. Ha ha.'

'They can't hear me, either,' said Dee. 'Only you can, because we are connected.'

I looked at her for just a second, maybe two, begging her to be quiet. Jess followed my stare.

'Are you waiting for someone?'

'No.'

'Do you expect something very exciting to happen in the kitchen in the next two minutes?'

'You could do some washing-up. That would be a miracle.'

Dad laughed, then stopped when Mum gave him a look. Jess snorted but went back to eating. I kept my eyes down, focused on the room. I could hear the fridge humming, the clock on the wall tick-tick-ticking.

'I like your family,' said Dee. She'd moved to stand behind me. I hadn't even noticed.

I nodded, only slightly, then turned it into scratching my ear.

'So,' said Mum, 'anything new with you guys?'

Jess and I looked at each other, and silence filled up the table.

I lay in bed and tried to clear my head. My phone was in my hand.

How will we even start? I typed. A minute passed, maybe less. My phone buzzed.

Investigate. Clues in the house? Internet. Library. Use yer head, dumbo.

Danny calling *me* dumbo. The world really had gone mad.

'Can you sense the book?' I said. 'Like, does it call to you, or shine in the dark or anything?'

Dee was sitting at my desk, staring out of the window at the sour-milk moon.

'I don't think that's how it works,' she said. 'I don't think that's how we work.'

'You don't know?'

She looked at me. Her eyes shone in the dark.

'This isn't ... me, Philippa. I don't look like this. I'm not normally like this at all. My own person, my own voice. I'm *part* of something, something vast and endless, something that rolls through time and space and binds every thing that ever lived. *That's* what I'm meant to be. Right now I'm a ... I'm a storm trapped in a photograph. I don't know. No, I can't sense the book.'

'I still don't get what you are,' I said. She smiled again, sadly, and slumped off the chair onto the floor.

'I'm a lost kid who needs to find my family.'

'You have Garth.'

'He's a lost kid too.'

'Oh.'

My phone buzzed again. *Going to sleep. Nite.*

Night night, I texted. I rubbed my eyes.

'Do you sleep?' I said.

'No.'

'Oh. Well, I do. So, y'know . . . '

'Yes,' said Dee, and then she turned back to the window, squinting, and jumped up.

'People!' she said. She darted forward, her body moving through my desk like it was nothing but mist, and glared into the night. 'I see them, nearby. They're driving this way!'

I jumped up from the bed, my phone bouncing off my duvet onto the carpet. 'What people? From the *house*?'

She nodded. She spoke quickly. 'I know their scent. Two of them. They were there.'

'Oh God, did they find us? Are they coming here?' Panic, hot and raw, gripped me. 'My family's here! And Danny – we have to tell Danny!'

I reached for my phone. My mouth was dry. 'Dee, where are they? How near? Tell me!'

She didn't answer. Her face was pressed against the glass, but it might as well have been empty air. I stepped forward and pulled a slither of curtain open. Outside was pitch black. My reflection stared back at me, alone in the room, pale and frightened. 'Dee, please,' I said, 'what do I do?'

She was frowning now, but something in my voice made her turn to me. When she spoke she sounded uncertain, and her eyes flicked back to the window. 'They are ... turning away. They're driving away.' She sounded confused. 'They are just ... passing by?'

'Bloody hell, you scared me,' I said.

She glared out into the dark. 'So close, so clueless. A coincidence that they came this way, I think.' She paused. 'They are bad people. Idiots.'

'But they don't know we're here?' I said. 'I need to know. Did they see us?'

Her eyes were like flames. 'No,' she said.

'You're sure?'

She moved forward again, and now she was moving through the wall, out into the freezing dark. 'I will follow—' she said.

'No!'

I reached out for her. She stopped and turned back to me. 'No?'

The panic was still there, like cold electricity inside me. 'I don't ... I don't want you to leave me here. Alone.'

'These people may lead me to the book, or—'

'But if you're not here I won't know if they – if others are ... '

Her expression was unreadable. 'I do not think—'

I had to make her understand. I was afraid there and then, my home suddenly a fortress under attack. I couldn't be alone and face what might come.

'If they're not coming here then we're safe for now, we can still find them, find the book, but they won't know where I live, where Mum and Dad and Jess and—'

She turned back to the window, her fingers twitching. 'They're leaving,' she said. 'I can barely ...' Then she sighed. 'You're right. I will stay. We should stick together, and running off ...' She trailed off and shook her head. She smiled weakly. 'Perhaps I was wrong. This house is safe. We will find the Society together.'

When I answered my voice was barely a whisper. 'Thank you.'

She looked at the wall and I pictured Danny so near and so far away. 'Garth doesn't seem to have seen them,' said Dee. She paused. Then, 'No need to tell him about this ... chance.'

'I'm sorry.'

She waved her hand at nothing, batting my words out the air. 'No, you're right, this should be done properly. I will stay.' She moved back into the room. 'You should sleep.'

'Um. Yeah. What if they come back, though?'

'I'll keep watch. I won't go far. Trust me.'

She smiled again and her eyes flashed, like acid fireflies frozen to the spot. 'I will protect you, Philippa,' she said.

94

Then she turned away again, her back to me, and watched the invisible night.

I dreamt I was flying through a world of dazzling Technicolor, of Van Gogh stars and *Wizard of Oz* roads. The smell of grass and apples and spices carried on the wind, and the water that frothed and foamed in the rivers was pure and icy and diamond-bright. The sky was black, or blue, and the shadows in the woods were filled with earth and secrets. I laughed and raced, faster than lightning, through it all, and I was happy, and I was free, and it was good.

A car horn melted through the morning air. I screwed up my eyes, then opened them and groaned. The horn sounded again, then someone shouted, and a dog barked. I stretched, rolled over, and looked at my phone.

'Morning,' said Dee. It sounded like a statement, not a greeting. 'It is raining. It's really grey.'

I froze, mid-stretch, and peered at her from behind my tangled hair.

'Oh,' I croaked. 'OK.'

'I didn't want to wake you. I have been quiet.'

'It's OK. I have to get up. School. I have school.'

I groaned again and pushed myself up off the pillows. I rubbed my eyes and tried, blearily, to focus on her. Was she angry? Had I ruined her hopes by being selfish, by being so damn childish? What would Danny have done? He probably would have run out into the night as well.

'I have to shower,' I said.

'I'll go downstairs. I think your mum's making . . . coffee?' She made the word sound like it was something new, some exotic spice to explore and kill for.

'Yeah. OK. So, I'll see you down there. Cool.'

She gave me a thumbs-up and left the room. I fell back into the bed, trying to think straight, trying to forget it all. I heard rain patter against the window and I wondered how this was going to end. I got up, showered, dressed and headed downstairs. Mum looked up when I walked into the kitchen. She'd been reading a magazine and I peered over her shoulder at the article.

'So,' I said, 'which of these seven ways to find a better man will you be using today?'

'Well, it's so hard to pick, isn't it? They're all so sure-fire.'

'Morning, Mum.'

'Morning, sweetie. Sleep OK?'

'Yup. Where's Dad?'

'Off to work already.'

'Ah, hence looking for a better model.'

'I'd take any model who'd have me,' she said, then laughed at her own joke.

'It's too early for jokes,' I said.

'I'm wasted here.'

'Well, send me a postcard when you jet off to your new life of hot models and stand-up tours.'

She tried to hit me with a tea towel, but I was too quick for her. I laughed and got myself a bowl of cereal. When I looked up, Dee was sitting opposite me.

'Bloody hell!' I said, jumping in surprise.

Mum sprang up. 'What, what?'

'Oh, I just ... remembered I had a project due. I forgot. Crap.'

She cocked her head, folding her arms. 'Oh, Philippa, really. You know how important homework is! If you just do a little every night ... '

'Yeah. You're right. Sorry. It's not due today, though. I have time. I'll do it.'

'Well, see you do. What subject?'

Dee was watching us, her face blank. I looked straight at her.

'Religious studies. Maybe some history, too.'

Mum sounded puzzled. 'They give you cross-subject projects?'

I took a bite of cereal. 'Apparently,' I said. I ate the rest of my breakfast in silence. Mum went back to her magazine.

Back up in my room, I started throwing books into my school bag.

'You can't just *apparate* like that!'

Dee frowned. 'Apparate?'

'It's from— Oh, never mind. You can't sneak up on me, my family's going to think I've lost it!'

She looked at her feet. 'Sorry. I'm still trying to work all this out.'

I grabbed my pencil case, searched around for my maths book. Dee looked suddenly miserable, and I paused, my anger melting away.

'I'm sorry. It's just been a weird few days.'

'I know you didn't ask for this.'

'Well, neither did you, right? You're just minding your own business doing ... whatever it is you do ... and then bang, you're dragged here, then shipwrecked.'

She looked thoughtful for a moment. 'Shipwrecked. Yes. That's a good way of saying it. And now I want to sail back!'

Neither of us spoke. The rain was getting heavier, the sky above a crinkled white plastic bag that rolled over the horizon. I reached for my phone and texted Danny. *See you in a bit? No playing sick today!*

It didn't take long for him to reply. *Sure thing. D x*

I smiled and looked at the girl.

'I had a weird dream last night,' I said. 'About that place you showed me. That in-between place.'

'The World Between,' she said.

'It was nice.'

'It's a powerful place. Lots of worlds connect, you know. It draws life from them, I guess. Strong place.'

'Can't you use it, then, to go where you want?'

Dee shook her head, her eyes darkening. 'Shipwrecked,' she said in a quieter, calmer voice. 'Putting your face under the water isn't the same as diving to the bottom.'

'Huh?'

'Garth and I tried. We tested this world, our new boundaries. Where we showed you and Danny – that's all we can do. Show. It's too far to actually step through. Pressing your face up against a window isn't the same as going through a door.'

'You like to speak in riddles, huh?'

She shrugged. 'It's easier than trying to make sense of it.'

The dog was barking outside again. I went to the window to see if I could see him, but the rain made everything a grey haze.

'Do you want to see it again?' she said.

'The World Between?'

'I could show you again, if you need more proof.'

I was excited and nervous. It was stupid and impossible. Other worlds? Spectres? I turned to her and smiled.

'You want to go?' she said.

I reached out and took her hand. 'I absolutely do.'

We were standing at the foot of the mountain now. It rose up behind us, impossibly tall, its rock a deep purple, its top lost in frozen wisps of snow and clouds. I stumbled, caught myself, felt my feet press into the grass and the rich, black earth beneath.

'You are OK?' said Dee. I took a deep breath – the air was cold and smelled like orange and mint and clove – and swallowed.

'All good.' I bent over, straightened up again. 'How do you do this? Are we really here?'

'Yes. No. You're still in your bedroom, I suppose. You've closed your eyes for a second and – bang! Here we are.'

'What if Mum walks in?'

'I suppose she'll think you're sleeping.'

I walked forward, away from the mountain. Pools of water were glistening in the light. Willow and pear trees grew in lazy, wonky circles around the water. At the edge of the grass the forest whispered.

'You're not really supposed to be here,' said Dee, 'but neither am I. A little compensation for what I'm going through, I think. Isn't it lovely?'

'It's the most beautiful thing I've ever seen.'

'Ha! I am glad. But we should be careful. Reality has to call you back at some point.'

'Does it?'

'School. Danny. Your family. The house by the sea. None of that's here, is it?'

'No ...'

'The furthest you could possibly be from home, and the nearest I can get, for now.'

I turned back to face her. The wind rustled my hair. Dee was staring out across the brilliant world.

'You've no idea what's out there,' she said.

'You could tell me.'

She smiled and shook her head. 'Some things are best as secrets and surprises.'

I took a step closer to the edge of the mountain path. Pebbles and dust moved beneath my feet. I felt my skin prickle, felt the fierce cold of the air in my lungs.

'This place,' I said, 'it's crazy. I can smell the wind. I can almost hear the stars as they sizzle!'

'Intense,' said Dee. 'Yes.'

I closed my eyes and breathed in again. The air was sweet. Rustles and whispers rolled through my head. I felt as if I were strong just for being here, that this place was worth more than every meal, every night's sleep I'd ever had.

'How can this not be a real place?' I said. Dee walked a few steps ahead of me and stared out through the trees.

'Threads that connect webs have their own beauty,' she said.

'Webs are made of threads,' I said.

'Language,' she said, waving her hand through the air. 'Like catching flies. You know what I mean?'

I thought that I did. I craned my neck up.

'No moon,' I said.

'Mmm.'

'But those stars – are they moving?'

Dee followed my gaze, turning lazily, like a cat already full of cream. She smiled. 'Not stars,' she said. 'Fireflies.'

As we watched, the sky above us, so still a moment ago, buzzed and flickered, like the sheen on a pond disturbed by a stone, the movement rippling out. Specks of light fell and crackled and filled the air around me, their movements impossibly fast. I was surrounded by white, pale yellow, acid green, soft blue, every colour blurring into one as the world became a perfect silent storm.

'Amazing things,' said Dee. 'Magic, really. Life at its best.'

I laughed and held out my hands, the fireflies always moving away just before I could touch them, like vapour more than anything, clouds of light that fled from me and filled any space as soon as I had moved on.

'Like shoals of fish,' I said.

'Swimming through the night. I like that.' Dee floated higher, joining the fireflies, tossing and turning in the air, and this crazy thought, that she could float, that she could fly, tumbled through my mind, overwhelmed by everything else.

'They don't fear me!' she laughed.

I stared up, at the fireflies that were stars, and the stars that were fireflies, at this impossible place, this World Between, where everything was bright, where everything seemed right.

'Go, silly babies, go!' shouted Dee, and she flung her arms up, brushing the fireflies as they raced along, higher, higher, leaving us behind, back up into the sky, to dance and burn and keep their mysteries. Dee was laughing as she landed next to me, her skin glowing, her hair waving in an impossible, invisible wind.

'Wonderful,' she said. 'Full of wonder. Oh, yes.'

'You like it here too,' I said. She bit her lip.

'I like feeling things,' she said. 'I like the experience. It's not something we have when we're . . . when I'm back where I should be.'

Her smile flickered. I looked down at the grass, at its full moss green. It had seemed so vivid before, but now, without the fireflies, even it seemed faded, just dull and normal and vague.

'Death,' I said.

'Yes.'

'You come for everyone.'

'That's how it works.'

I paused. 'Even me?'

She met my eyes. I saw power in hers, fire and light and galaxies burning in seconds. What did she see in mine?

'Death is not unnatural,' she said. 'It goes with being born. Trust me, Philippa. I know what I'm saying, for once. When it comes, don't try to run. Don't try to *fight*. That's what the Society's doing. Fighting against the dark because they can't see the light around them. I wish they could. It would hurt less, if they would just stop running.'

'But—'

She shook her head. 'Death isn't cruel. The world is good. Cling to that. Please.'

A single firefly had fallen down, landing on the grass, its light burning, fading, burning, fading. Dee watched it with eyes that seemed to stare into eternity.

'We should go back,' she said, 'or your mum really will come and find you. OK?'

'I'd be fine with that.'

'She might think you're in a coma.'

'Worse things have happened.'

She smiled, a little nervous, and reached out for my hand.

'A little at a time,' she said. 'OK? We should get back.'

Slowly, sadly, I let my fingers touch hers. All the colour drained from the world, and the sound of rain on dirty glass rose up and met us like a wave. I was in my bedroom, my throat dry, my eyes watering.

'Philippa, Jess, I can drive you if you want?' Mum was shouting. 'But I have to leave in five minutes!'

Paul Baxter was leaning against the wall, a toothpick in his mouth like some sort of skinny-ass cowboy. He smirked when he saw me and said something to his friends. They giggled and prodded each other.

'Phil the Thrill! Up for some fun?'

A girl walking past – Win-Yan, I think her name was – gave him a dirty look. I rolled my eyes and ignored him.

'Come on, so choosy?' he called. I thought of what Danny had said, and tried to hide my smile.

'That boy is unfriendly,' said Dee. She was walking just behind me, her mouth open as she gawped and stared at the hive of the school. Kids ran, teachers shouted, everything smelled of the rain and mud and sweat. I shifted the bag on my shoulder and pulled my phone out of my pocket, putting it to my ear without dialling anyone.

'He's just a jerk,' I said. 'He thinks it's fun to make kids feel bad.'

She frowned and shook her head. 'That won't end well.'

'I hope that's a promise.'

'Buy one get one free?' said Paul, raising his voice. A few kids looked at him, some laughed, most tried to pretend they hadn't heard him. I lowered my head and muttered, 'Just keep going, ignore him, not today.'

'You do not like him,' said Dee.

I snorted. 'That's one way to put it.'

'He upsets you,' she said.

'Well, yeah, sometimes, but—'

'Wait here,' said Dee. 'I want to try something.'

I didn't even pretend to talk into the phone. 'Wait, what? Dee, what are you—'

She turned and walked slowly up to the group of boys. It freaked me out how none of them saw her, how their eyes didn't even register her standing there. They saw me, though, and thought I was looking at them. Asif Malik – lanky, too

105

much hair gel – made a kissy sound and thrust towards me. The others cackled on cue.

'No,' said Dee. 'You shouldn't. Here.'

She reached forward and put her hands on either side of Paul's face. His expression flickered, like a sudden doubt had taken hold, or a piece of ice had fall down his back.

'Be afraid,' said Dee, straining a little, the tip of her tongue poking out. Then, with a small gasp, Paul Baxter stumbled back, the pick falling from his lips. He put his hands to the side of his face, and lowered his head.

'I want my mummy,' he said. The guys laughed at first, trying to play along with a joke they didn't get, but that trickled into nothing. Paul looked at them, every hint of humour gone.

'I'm scared of the monster! I want my mummy!'

Were those tears in his eyes? He pushed a couple of the guys – Philip Choi, someone I didn't know – and stumbled forward, then called out, loud enough that everyone stopped to look.

'Where's Mummy? I want her!'

Other kids started laughing, confused, some nervous. Paul Baxter ran. The rain hadn't stopped, but he burst out of a side door, never even flinching, and into the storm, his backpack still on the ground in the hallway. Nobody moved.

'What the hell?' said Asif. I turned away, my phone back by my ear, waiting for Dee to wander back over.

'What the hell did you do?' I hissed.

'Played around. A little. It is not difficult. Don't worry, he'll be fine. I just showed him something scary.'

'What, like you?'

She didn't say anything, but her eyes flashed like lightning.

'Come on,' I said. 'I don't want to get caught up in this.'

'He won't bother you anymore.'

I put my phone away, looking up and down the hallway for Danny or Garth.

'Well, that's good,' I said quietly. 'I think. Maybe. Just be careful. OK?'

'OK.'

I smiled. 'That was kind of cool, I guess. "Where's my mummy?" Nice.'

Dee did a little bow and we carried on walking.

The day crawled past. Maths, history, double English – more *Lord of the Flies* – and finally lunch. The rain had stopped, the clouds thinning out so at least some light could get through. Raindrops dripped off leaves, but as soon as we could, everyone burst outside. Being trapped in school is bad enough, but being trapped in a school that smells of wet blazers is worse.

'We just need to get together and think this through,' I said. 'We can do it. We can.'

'You seem odd speaking to yourself,' said Dee.

'I'm speaking to you!'

A girl I didn't know – a Year Seven, judging by her size – looked at me in surprise, and scurried past.

'Others won't see it that way,' said Dee, and she smiled.

I cleared my throat and lowered my voice. 'This just gets better. Now I look like I'm losing it.'

'Hmm,' she said, and she floated in front of me. We carried on walking, me dodging puddles, Dee watching the world around her, the other kids, the teachers marching past. She cocked her head like a puzzled dog but kept her mouth shut.

'Where's Danny got to?' I said. 'Can't you just— Wait!'

I froze, taking a quick step back and ducking down behind clump of bushes. Dee frowned and moved towards me.

'Problem?' she said, sounding amused.

'Shh! Listen – it's them!'

Her face dropped, her eyes hardening. 'The Society? Where? I—'

'No, no,' I said, waving my hand. 'Listen, around the corner. It's Danny and his mates. It's them!'

For a second she didn't move, and her eyes glowed with power. Then, with a confused smile, she moved to sit next to me as I pushed myself further behind the bush, my back scratching against the brick wall.

'And you're hiding because . . . ?'

'I just . . . can't with those guys right now, OK?'

She nodded, shrugged, and was silent. As I hugged my knees to my chest, feeling the damp ground soak into my trousers, the guys came round the corner, laughing and loud, Danny right there with them. Scott Haycott was saying something, the others listening, and I held my breath as they came to a stop.

'I swear, just like that, and then he ran off!'

'No way,' said one of the others. 'You're making this up.'

'Piss off, am not.'

Philip Choi shook his head. 'He'll have you for laughing at him.'

'Yeah, yeah,' said Scott. He cracked his knuckles. 'Weird, though, right?'

I looked at Dee. She looked back, impassive.

'So he just acted strange?' said Danny. I tried to see his face through the bushes.

'Maybe he's cracked.' That was Asif.

'I'm sure it's nothing. Just Paul being Paul. Good way to get out of classes, eh?'

'You think?'

'Yeah,' said Danny. He kicked at a stone on the ground. 'Yeah. Whatever. Forget it. You guys up to much later?'

'Maybe. Paul's still pissed at you, you know.'

'For taking the mick cause Kasia wouldn't give him one? I only knew cause you told me.'

Scott laughed. 'Just make it up to him or something. We're a team. Got to get on.'

'If it'll make him feel better, *I'll* make out with him,' said Danny, and they all laughed. Asif put his arm around Danny.

'Then at least someone would, eh?'

'Oh, maybe I should tell Paul *you* said that!' said Scott.

'Fine! He's lost it, anyway. Need a new captain if he keeps on being a nutter.'

Danny tried to sound bored, but he couldn't keep the worry out of his voice. 'So he just ... suddenly changed?'

The guys shrugged, grunted.

'And no one was there, touching him or—'

'Touching him, eh?' said Asif.

'Shove off. You know what I meant.'

'Nope,' said Scott, 'just us. I mean, a few kids were around. Your Phil was there, she'd have seen it, so you can ask her – you know, if you're not too busy ... '

'Watch it,' said Danny, and now he sounded serious. 'No more jokes. None of that. Grow up, guys. OK?'

The guys smiled, but no one argued. Philip Choi pulled out his phone.

'No plans later then, yeah?'

'Weather's rubbish,' said Asif. 'Probably just go home and watch TV.'

'We know what you'll be watching, you loser!'

They laughed again, Danny with them, and I prayed they wouldn't find me, wouldn't look in this direction.

'Where's Garth got to?' whispered Dee. 'He shouldn't have left him alone.'

'Shh!' I said. 'Danny can hear you too, remember?'

There was someone else with them now, a boy I hadn't

seen before. They guys smiled when they saw him. 'All right, Smithy!' said Danny. 'How's it going?'

'Not bad, not bad. Just been with Daisy.'

The guys crowded round him, grins on their faces. 'Oh yeah? Been with, eh?'

Smithy held up his hands. 'It's not like me to kiss and tell,' he said, and they laughed again. Dee sighed. 'This world is so ... complex,' she said. 'Things always have so many meanings.'

'Does he mean Daisy McNair?' I muttered.

Dee looked at me and back at the boys.

'So much confusion,' she said, and she moved a bit closer to me. The guys were walking again, off away from our hiding place, and the sounds of their jeers and jokes echoed among the buildings.

'You never did!' said Scott.

'Go on,' said Danny, 'go on, you have to tell us. Go on, Smithy!'

'You're one to talk!'

'Ah, shut up and tell. No changing the subject.'

Their voices faded away, and then we were alone again. Awkwardly, my muscles already sore from tensing, I crawled back out from behind the bush.

'Elegant,' said Dee.

I picked bits of leaf from my hair. 'Oh, shut up. Come on. If we're going to find this book of yours we still need to talk to Danny, just when he's alone. He knows that.'

'Why hide then?'

I had spider web on my blazer and mud on my trousers. My butt was sore and damp and my head hurt. 'I don't know,' I said. 'Come on. Just . . . be quiet for a bit, please?'

She shrugged, nodded, and fell in behind me. I was angry at myself, and confused, and sad, but that had to wait. We had other problems.

We found Danny and Garth by one of the science huts. The other guys were gone. They looked like they were arguing, but as soon as they noticed us they stopped, stiffened up, grinned.

'Still putting up with her, then?' said Garth.

'She's handy with the lads,' I said. Danny frowned, like he was solving a puzzle, then looked at me.

'I knew it! You did something to Paul, right?'

'I didn't do anything!'

'I might have,' said Dee.

Danny scowled. 'Phil, he's my friend.'

'Philippa,' I said.

'Fine! Sorry! But seriously, man. What'd you do?'

'Nothing more than a nightmare,' said Dee. 'He was being rude.'

'He's always rude, that's his thing!'

'That's not a *thing*, Danny. It's just dumb. Everyone thinks so.'

'Everyone, eh?'

We were on the edge of an argument again, a great black hole that would swallow everything. I sensed it, tried to pull back, like pulling a galloping horse to a stop.

'It wasn't ... planned. I'm sorry. He'll be fine though, right, Dee?'

Dee looked at Garth, who raised his eyebrows but said nothing. 'Yes,' she said. 'I wouldn't have *hurt* him.'

'The guys might,' said Danny, folding his arms. 'You have to keep up your image, y'know? This is rough. Taking the piss when he's not there is one thing, but this – It's not fair, Phil.'

The black hole was right there, and I held it back behind my teeth. I swallowed my words – not fair? For *Paul*? After what he said? – and took a deep breath, counting to five, feeling the cold breeze kiss my cheeks.

'OK,' I said. 'Focus. Garth and Dee. The book. Remember?'

Danny still looked angry. 'Yeah, I remember.' He shoved his hands in his pockets. 'So,' he said, 'what's the plan?'

'Finding the book is important,' said Dee. 'For two reasons, really. Getting us home' – she nodded at Garth, who winked back – 'and stopping this Society from doing any real damage. Do you know how close they got? It's too dangerous.'

'What would someone even do with ... with Death?' said Danny. Bursts of weak sunlight were lighting up the buildings behind us. The sound of kids running and shouting mingled with the hum of traffic.

'Bad things,' said Garth. 'Take out enemies, live forever, who knows? It can't happen.'

'Why does the book even exist?'

'Because people are greedy and don't know what's good for them.'

Dee shook her head. 'I think it's that once you get a taste, it's hard to give it up. Magic. Spirits. Spectres. You guys know we're out there now – would you go back to being like everybody else?'

We looked at each other. I remembered the smell of the spiced wind, the colour of the sky of the World Between. Danny looked at his feet.

'We're not *bad*, though,' he said.

Dee smiled and said nothing.

'So,' said Garth, letting the word drag out in the silence, 'finding the book. How do we do this?'

'We can't touch things,' said Dee. 'So it has to be you. We need to know who those people are. Do you know them? Where did they come from? We have to find them.'

I puffed out my cheeks, stretched my fingers back against my palms. Danny laughed nervously. 'We didn't know them at all,' he said. 'Right, Phil?'

'Strangers,' I said, 'but we did hear their names. What was it – Susan? Cully. Some others. George, maybe?'

'I don't know,' said Danny.

'Definitely Susan. But there are hundreds of Susans. Thousands. There are two in my class.'

'It probably wasn't Susan Skipper,' said Danny. 'Susan O'Brien, though, she always gives me the creeps.'

'Only since she said no to you at the Year Seven disco.'

He opened his mouth to protest, decided against it, shoved his hands deeper into his pockets.

'Whatever,' he said.

Dee and Garth watched us with shining eyes.

'Cully,' said Danny. 'I've not heard that before. There can't be a lot of those.'

'So we . . . look them up? Do phone books still exist?'

Danny shook his head. 'Those are last names, anyway. You think it's a last name?'

'Maybe? We could search for it and see if anything comes up.'

I pulled out my phone and tried it out.

'Damn,' said Danny, looking at the screen. '859,000 results?'

'It's a town in Switzerland,' I said, flicking through the pages. 'This is useless.'

'Try Cully and Baymouth together.'

I typed, turning so we could all see the screen.

'It's just a load of rubbish,' said Danny.

He was right. The results were nonsense – companies, pictures of foreign places, pages in languages I couldn't read . . .

'How about the police?'

Danny frowned. 'Report them? They'd lock us up as loons.'

'No, I mean, what if we asked them to search their database. They must have one, one the public can't get, with people's names and addresses. If we went and pretended we had to find our, I don't know, our uncle, and we knew his name but not where he was . . .'

'Just his first name?'

'You're children,' said Garth, folding his arms but looking thoughtful. 'You could play innocent. Perhaps they would be open to it?'

'With a bit of persuasion,' said Dee. She flexed her fingers. Garth's face darkened. 'We shouldn't,' he said.

'Huh. She already did,' I said, nodding at Dee and looking down at my phone.

'And she was wrong to do that,' said Garth. He sounded suddenly older, almost angry, his eyes darkening, his voice getting deeper. 'It's dangerous, to play with their minds. You know this.'

Dee cocked her head. 'We're only here because humans tried to play with us.'

'Not these,' said Garth, spreading his arms up to waved at the school, the groups of kids standing around. 'They're not all the same. Be careful, Dee.'

'Is Paul going to be OK?' said Danny.

'Oh, he'll be fine,' I said.

He looked at me and pulled a face. 'How would you know? Dee, is Paul OK?'

She waved his question from the air. 'I told you, he'll be fine.'

'We shouldn't mess,' said Garth. 'We should just get back as quick as we can.'

For a moment I thought Dee would argue, but she held her tongue, nodding as if she agreed. The four of us stood in awkward silence. Over on the field someone shouted out, someone shouted back. A bird was singing up in the trees.

'It should be you,' said Danny.

'Huh?'

'Who goes to the police, I mean. Play nice, you know. Say you're lost and need help.'

'Why should it be me?'

He looked surprised. 'You're the girl.'

'I'm "the girl"? So I'm meant to be all lost and lonely?'

He rolled his eyes, looking up into the needly branches of the trees. 'You know what I meant. It makes sense.'

I knew it did, but that annoyed me.

'The police can't help,' I said. It sounded so grown-up, so certain. I hoped my voice wasn't shaking. Dee nodded and sucked on her lip.

'We don't know enough,' she said.

'Then we have to go back,' said Danny. We all looked at him.

'Back?' said Dee.

'To the house. Where they did it, where it went down. We have to investigate. It's the only way. You know I'm right.'

I pulled a face. 'What would we find, though? Their evil plan typed up and laminated?'

Danny rolled his eyes and turned away, looked up at the sky, back at me. 'We don't know if we don't try,' he said. 'It's literally the only thing we have right now – that house, the fact they chose it, they went there, spent time there.'

Nobody spoke. A few kids ran past and we moved further into the shadows of the trees that grew along the edge of the school.

'He's right,' said Garth. He looked at Dee and shrugged his shoulders. 'You can't fault him on that.'

'I don't like it,' she said. 'It seems risky.'

'Couldn't we call someone, leave a tip, we could be anonymous, we could—'

'Say what?' said Danny. He was getting angry now, the red in his cheeks getting darker. 'That we saw someone doing something, but we can't say what, so we need them to go to the house and look for something, but we can't say why, and then we want them to tell us, but we can't say who we are?'

Garth laughed and moved closer to Danny. Dee raised her eyebrows and looked between him and me. The air felt heavy, like a storm was waiting, begging for a spark. I put up my hands.

'Fine. You're right. It makes sense and it's worth a shot. We'll go back to the house. Makes a change, doesn't it? You convincing me to go.'

'Very funny,' said Danny, but he didn't even smile. He

looked at his phone, looked over my shoulder. 'I just want to check on Paul,' he said. Dee opened her mouth to say something but Danny shook his head, pocketing his phone in one smooth movement. 'We can go tonight,' he said. 'I'll make an excuse. Meet by the gates, yeah? Make sure you're not followed, though. Five o'clock sound good?'

I stared at him. I stumbled over my words. 'Y-yeah. Sure. Cool. Five.'

He nodded, looked up once at Dee, then walked off, calling Garth without looking back. Garth looked at the ground, floating slowly away.

'Sorry,' he mumbled over his shoulder. Dee smiled weakly and waved one hand. She looked at me, nervous, like someone crouching to pet a wild cat. 'So . . . ' she said.

'You heard him. Five o'clock. Don't want to be late, do we? Might get detention.'

'He's angry,' said Dee. 'But not at you, I think. Things will work out.'

'We'll see,' I muttered. Some kids nearby were playing, screaming, laughing with each other. I rolled my eyes and walked away.

I've always loved the ocean. There's something vast about it, about how it stretches away to the horizon, down to the depths, away to other worlds. I imagine myself, one small speck on a map, lost against its rolling, roaring waves. The ocean makes me feel things. It makes me small and alive. Listening to the waves as they crashed into the cliffs, I couldn't help feeling nervous. We were too exposed here, standing on the strip of dirt in front of the fence. If those people came back, if they drove up, if they saw us . . .

'Calm down,' I said. I kicked at the sandy dirt with my heel.

'I can't see anyone,' said Dee. She was staring out at the town, her back to the house, squinting and watching. She perked up. 'Except Danny. He's heading this way.'

I checked my phone. 'Late,' I said.

'Mmm.'

'This is going to be a waste of time.'

A seagull circled above, shrieking and diving. I took a deep breath and smelled the sea. I wasn't going to fight with him, but if he wanted to be a dick . . .

'There,' said Dee, and she pointed down the path. Danny was cycling towards us, the bike swaying from side to side slightly as he pushed himself to speed up the hill. I smiled. He was always trying to show off.

'This could be helpful,' said Dee. 'We don't know yet.'

'OK, I get it,' I said. 'We're all friends again. Thank you.'

'You people are strange,' she said, but came to stand next to me as we watched the boys approach. Danny skidded as he turned, a wave of dust puffing up from the wheels. I waved my hand in front of my face as he jumped off, panting slightly.

'Late,' he said. 'Sorry.'

Garth nodded his head at Dee. Neither of them spoke. I wondered if they even needed to.

'Well, you're here,' I said. 'That's the important thing, yeah?' A break in the clouds let the sun fall on my face. It felt warm and my mood lifted a bit. 'Ready to explore the house?'

'They're not here, right?' Danny said. He was looking at Dee and I felt a pang of anger. I balled my fists. We weren't going to fight.

'The house is empty,' she said. 'Just ghosts and memories.'

Danny pulled a face. 'That was ... creepy. Thanks.'

'You're welcome.'

Out in the water, unseen, a ship sounded its horn. The noise was sudden, jarring, and it seemed to wake Danny up. 'Good. OK. Let's go in. We need to look for anything – bits of paper, a receipt, any clothes, any food. They can all be clues.'

He had his breath back now. 'OK?' he said again.

'Absolutely. I love that you've gone all ... Sherlock Holmes.'

I picked up my schoolbag and we started walking down the path towards the house. It seemed like years ago we'd last been here. Dee and Garth held back, moved closer together, whispering their own secrets. I looked sideways at Danny, at the sparse hair on his chin, at the way he still looked so young, so like the boy I'd played make-believe with. He looked at me and frowned, but it was curious, not angry.

'What? Trying to work out how I can be this damn hand-some and still hang out with you? I know it's a mystery. I think it's my sheer kindness, kind of like charity work, you know?'

I snorted. 'It's amazing how someone so humble can also be so rugged. Tell me, do you work out?'

He flexed his arm. 'What do you think?'

I felt something relax inside me. This was how it should be. This was the real Danny.

'Do you remember playing Cluedo in Scotland?' I said.

'In Edinburgh? Yeah. Man, that was, what, ten years ago?'

'Bit less than that. We went just before my eleventh birth-day. Five years ago. '

Danny puffed out his cheeks. 'Five years? Really? Seems like—'

'A lot longer? Yeah. You remember it, though?'

He nodded and shoved his hands in his pockets. 'That rain, man. Every bloody day. I mean, Edinburgh's nice but that was just ridiculous.'

'We played Cluedo for, like, three days. You kept cheating.'

He looked indignant. 'I did not!'

'You did! You looked at my cards in the mirror. You made sure you sat opposite every time.'

The ship horn was blasting again. The sound echoed, fainter and fainter. Danny opened his mouth, closed it, his eyes suddenly wide. 'I did cheat! Hell, I'd forgotten that. The mirror, you're right!'

'You still lost.'

'I was ten!'

'So was I.'

He looked at me and shook his head. 'You were probably cheating, too. Such a sneak. Good thing it wasn't for money.'

'You don't play Cluedo for money. And if we had, I would have owned you.'

We walked on. The house was dark – a dead, broken thing perched on the edge of the world.

'Edinburgh,' said Danny. 'What made you think of that?'

I shrugged. 'Cluedo. Clues. What we're doing now. I don't know.'

I looked away and let my mind wander. Edinburgh had been a family trip, and Danny counted as family. We'd stayed in Old Town, in a flat filled with books and games and the collected things of a thousand travellers: pine cones and postcards and spoons and hats and forgotten, faded photos. I'd loved it. We all had. The rain had hardly mattered. Mum played records on the scratchy old record player and Dad made pancakes. We'd looked out over the rooftops of the city at night and made up stories of all the lights we could see.

'We should go back,' I said. Danny knocked his shoulder in to mine.

'You softy,' he said. Then, quieter, 'I'd like that.'

'Only if it's sunny,' I said.

'Deal. When it's sunny in Scotland, we'll live there for a

month.' The thought made me happy. 'But no cheating at games,' I added.

'I make no promises. May the best man win.'

We'd made it to the house, now. The door was open, its hinges bent and broken. *Like a mouth without a tooth*, I thought, and my skin felt prickly as we stepped inside. It was colder in here – the dark and the shadows made it feel like night.

'Here you go, guys,' said Danny, stepping aside and calling back to Garth and Dee. 'Welcome home. It's been too long, yeah?'

The spectres looked grim, almost wary, as they entered. Garth pointed to the floor, to the scuffed chalk, the scratches and marks. 'They've removed the symbols,' he said.

'Isn't that good?'

'We might have been able to copy. It could have helped us get back.'

Dee's voice was gentle when she spoke. 'We need to stop them doing it again, though, first. Once we know the Society has been stopped, we can think of home.'

Garth's face had darkened. 'This place isn't home,' he said to Danny. 'This is where we were pulled from our home by dark magic, carved from our family like meat from a carcass.'

The room was silent. Danny looked at his feet.

'I'm sorry,' I said. 'We didn't mean—'

'You can't understand,' said Dee, 'and that's fine. We know you're helping. It's just . . . imagine your hand was cut off. Would it be pleased to return to the butcher's block?'

'My hand doesn't have a life of its own,' said Danny.

'I thought a growing boy's hand was his very best friend?' I said. Danny's cheeks flushed and I tried to hide my smile. 'Come on,' I said. 'Search. Let's be quick. I don't like it here, either.'

'We can start upstairs,' said Dee. 'You two start down here.'

'Uh, right. Yeah. Cool.' Danny cleared his throat and straightened his jacket. 'Come on, Garth. Kitchen.'

As I headed up the stairs I couldn't help laughing.

Half an hour later we were standing back in the main room, dusty and empty handed. If there was anything to find, the Society hadn't made it easy. 'They washed the floor with water,' said Garth. 'And there's a smell, something sweet, on the doors.'

'Polish,' said Danny. 'I think they wiped away any prints.'

'Who do they think we are, the police?'

I was annoyed again. This whole thing was a waste of time, and Dee and Garth were jumpy.

'They don't know who you are,' said Dee, 'but it's a sensible precaution, really. You already know too much, don't you?'

'Don't be so dramatic,' said Danny.

'Don't tell Dee what to do!' I said. He looked at me and sighed.

'We know they are worried,' said Garth. 'Worry makes people careless, doesn't it?'

'Sure,' I said. Danny shrugged.

'We should rest and think,' said Garth.

'You just want to get out of here,' said Danny.

Around us the house was dark and watchful. The light outside was fading, gloom covering the town. The smell of the ocean wafted in. The cold of the water made me shiver.

'Let's head home,' I said. No one responded. The air felt thick with a failure we couldn't pin down. 'Come on,' I said again. 'No point moping around here. I'm getting chilly.'

Dee was by my side. 'You're right. Of course. Let's go.'

Slowly, wary now every sound seemed to fill the darkening world, we made our way out of the house, away from the cliff, back towards the gates at the end of the path. Dee and Garth hung back again, talking in whispers and gestures. Danny walked beside me saying nothing.

'It was a good idea,' I tried. He clicked his tongue, spat on the ground.

'Nice,' I said.

'We're back to square one. How are we meant to find them now?'

'Honestly? I don't know.'

We kept walking. I wished I knew what to say. Danny always seemed so ready to be angry, like he was hovering on the edge of something, holding back without even knowing it. I thought about what Jess had said – maybe guys really did grow up slower. It didn't seem right. It didn't seem fair.

Behind us, Dee and Garth stopped talking, their words breaking off in a single moment. Danny turned.

'What?' he said.

Garth was frowning, peering past us, down towards the town, where Danny's bike was still lying on its side. His eyes grew suddenly wider.

'We have to go. Now,' said Dee.

'What? Why?' I said.

'Because that's one of them! Run!'

Dee was already moving as she pointed to a figure running up the road towards us. They were too far away to be clear, about as far away from the gate as we were. It didn't take long to work out we were trapped.

'If we run, we're running towards them!' shouted Danny.

'If you don't get past the gate, you'll be stuck here for sure,' said Garth. He looked at the figure, looked back at Danny. 'They're old, moving slow. You're faster. Run, Danny!'

I was already moving, my schoolbag slapping awkwardly on my back as I picked up speed. I heard Danny behind me, saw the flash of Dee as she zipped ahead, like a humming-bird, like lightning.

'Idiot,' Danny spat. He was next to me now, a grim scowl on his face. 'Idiot! Of course they were watching. Run, Phil, come on!'

'I *am*!' I said. He was getting faster, leaving me behind,

and then he was at the gate, pushing through, turning back to me and shouting.

'That doesn't help!' I spat as I skidded to a halt, clambering through, my mind buzzing with panic.

'Come on, come on!' said Garth. We could see the man more clearly now. He was running towards us, his face red, one hand pressed to his ear.

'Phone. He's calling for help,' said Danny. He looked at me, his cheeks flushed. He took a deep breath. 'Shit,' he said.

'You have to get away,' said Dee. Then, 'They can't know about us.'

The man was getting nearer. Danny faced him, raised his fists.

'Don't be an idiot,' I said. I pulled his bike from the dirt. 'Ride! I'll get on the back.'

He pulled a face. 'They'll catch us,' he said.

'No they won't. You can do it. We can do it.'

The man was slowing down. He faced us, our backs against the dead end of the house. The only way back to the town was the road he was standing on.

'Children!' he shouted. 'I think we need to talk, hmm?'

'Let me at him,' said Garth, but Dee shook her head.

'If they're in danger, we stay with them,' she said. 'We're bound, remember? That means something.'

For a second – just a second – I thought that Garth might argue. Instead, he looked at Danny, at this pale, scared boy, and he nodded.

'With them,' he said.

'Good. Now let's *go*,' I said. The man had taken more steps towards us now. He smiled, his face shining with sweat, and held his hands open, as if he were inviting us to hug him.

'Kids,' he said. 'Please, let's just wait. There may have been a misunderstanding. When we carried out our little circus act – our trick the other night – if only we'd known you were there!' He chuckled, and his eyes met mine. 'Maybe we should have charged! It was a good show, yes?'

'Liar!' shouted Danny.

'Danny, don't,' said Dee.

I don't even know if Danny heard her. 'We know what you were doing. Magic! Summoning Death! Trying to *catch* it? You're mental. You're dangerous. And we heard you – you've killed people!'

The man's face was frozen in a curious smile, but his eyes hardened, and he took another step forward.

'Danny . . . ' said Garth.

'Now why would you say that?' said the man. 'Who would tell you that?'

No one spoke. Danny was panting, his cheeks spotted with red. Dee moved closer to me. 'Please,' she said, 'don't tell them anything else.'

'And don't use your names!' said Garth. He was in front of Danny now, his voice quiet, the kind you use for a spooked animal. 'We have to go before the Society gets here,' he said. 'OK? We'll ride your bike. Pick it up. Come on.'

'Oh, I'll do it,' I said, and I leaned down and reached for the handles.

There was a flicker in the air, and the man was beside me, his hand on my shoulder, the other pulling the bike away.

'I don't think so,' he said.

'Hey!'

A blur of movement, a strangled cry, and the man was on the ground, one hand clasped to his face. Danny was next to me, cradling his fist, his face twisted in anger. 'Don't you ever touch her,' he said, and with a jerk he pulled the bike from me. 'Get on,' he said, swinging his leg over and straightening the wheel.

'Nice one!' said Garth. Dee looked worried.

'You bloody maniacs!' spat the man. He sat up, wincing as he touched his swelling eye. 'This isn't some stupid game! Who did you tell? What do you know?'

'Bite me,' said Danny, and as I jumped on the back, gripping his shoulders as tight as I could, he kicked off, pedalling madly, spraying the man with gravel. He growled, a wild, terrible noise, and lunged at us. I screamed, tried to duck, but he had my bag, pulling me backwards.

'No!' I yelled. 'Let go! Danny!'

'Get off her!' he shouted, and we pulled forward, Danny leaning his weight on the pedals as I gripped him as tight as I could. My mind was panic and fear and noise. Dee was saying something, shouting something, and Danny was swearing and straining, and then there was a tear, a

130

snap, and we lurched forward, so hard I thought I would fall, be trampled, and I gripped Danny even closer. We were racing now, moving dangerously fast down the hill, Danny's legs pumping as he pushed the bike faster, faster. Wind whipped my hair, tore screams from my mouth, rattled my teeth. Then Dee was there, keeping pace, hovering, talking to me, saying something over and over. I looked at her, tried to make sense, turned my head back to look for the man.

'He's not chasing you. Philippa, he's not chasing.'

Dee was staring at me, waving her hand in front of my face. 'Do you understand?' she said. 'He's not coming after you.'

'Danny!' I shouted. He slowed, took a corner with a skid, kept moving.

'Danny!'

'What?'

'Slow down! He's not here!'

He turned to look back and the bike wobbled. I gripped his waist again, squeezing closer.

'Ow!' he said.

'I'm going to fall off!'

He swore again, squeezed the brakes, and we shuddered to a halt. I knew the street – it wasn't too far from home. Danny was panting, his face red, his neck pulsed as his heart raced.

'What – the – hell?' he said.

Garth was there beside him, and he moved closer, staring at Danny, whispering something. Dee faced me.

'He was one of them,' she said.

'Gee, you think?'

'I do,' she said.

I groaned. 'Sarcasm, Dee,' I said. 'Of course he was one of them! God, we're such idiots. That was too close. Too bloody close.'

Danny stood up straight. His eyes blazed with anger. 'Did he hurt you?' he said.

'I don't think—'

'Did he hurt you?' he shouted.

'Danny! No! Look, I'm OK, I'm OK. Are you?'

He ran his hands through his hair, paced back and forth. 'Oh, man,' he said. 'Oh, man, oh man. Yeah, yeah, I'm fine. I'm fine. If he hurt you, if he *touched* you—'

'Look, I'm all fine. But he— Oh, damn.'

Danny stepped closer, his movements sudden, jittery. 'What? What?'

'Look,' I said, holding up my bag, showing him the front. 'He ripped it! He tore the whole front pocket off.'

'He's a maniac!' said Danny, his voice cracking with anger, his breathing fast and shallow.

'I should have seen him coming,' said Dee. She was hovering at eye level, flitting back and forth like a panicked bird. 'I was distracted, I was . . . I don't know. I should have seen him coming.'

132

'But we're safe, we got away,' I said. Danny made a scoffing sound.

'We did,' I said. 'He can't have followed us. He won't know where we are.'

'But we need to know where he is, where they are,' said Garth. 'We're meant to be hunting them.'

'We need to take them by surprise,' said Dee. 'They are dangerous, remember? As Danny pointed out—'

'Why'd you have to annoy him like that?' I said. 'This isn't a game, Danny, it's not funny to—'

'I know it's not a game! What I said was true. You heard them in the house. They killed people. They know we know. That's why they're after us. Maybe we *should* go to the police.'

I looked at Dee. 'No,' I said, 'no, we can't. That would just make it even harder to help these guys.'

'We're asking a lot,' said Garth. 'I know that. I'm sorry. But—'

'We'll find a way,' said Danny. He was watching Garth, fiddling with the zip on his coat.

'We should go,' he said. 'Phil, you OK getting home?'

'Uh, yeah.'

'Good. Good. You coming, Garth?'

For a moment, I thought Garth might argue, want to track the Society, want to do something. Instead, he nodded and turned to leave. His dark skin almost merged with the growing dark.

'I'll see you tomorrow,' said Danny. 'Get home safe. Don't stay out.'

He grabbed his bike, swung on, and was off. In a few seconds he was gone, Garth with him, the evening suddenly full of a terrible nothing.

'That was weird,' I said. Dee pulled a face.

'We probably should get going,' she said, looking back down the road, back towards the house by the cliff.

'People need to stop telling me what to do,' I said, but I knew she was right, and I started walking the way Danny had just cycled.

'Do you think those guys are up to something?' I said.

'I think,' said Dee, 'that the more I'm here, the less I understand. I'm glad you're all right, though.'

I laughed, holding up my bag. 'Can't say the same for this poor thing.'

'A part of it ripped away,' she said. 'I know how it feels.'

'Oh, God,' I said, and we both laughed then, two broken losers walking through the gloom.

SEVEN

I SAT IN bed that night, Dee hovering near the window, my phone in my hand. I flicked through messages, old pictures, stupid jokes.

Danny was playing music. I could hear the *thump, thump* of bass muffled by the wall.

Oi, I texted, *turn it down. I'm going to bed. Night xx*

Someone knocked on my door. Dee turned, lazily, and then looked back out of the window. 'Jess,' she said. 'I'll let you two talk.'

She moved forward, more mist than girl, and passed through the wall, out into the dark.

'Thanks,' I whispered as I swung my legs out of bed.

'Is that you, revered sister?'

Jess pushed the door open, her hair still damp from the shower. She smelled of apple and mint, of being clean and calm.

'So respectful,' she said. 'I'm worried. Where's the body?'

'They'll never find 'em. What's up?'

I pulled the covers over me again, plugging my phone in and straightening the pillows. Jess pulled the chair from my desk and spun it to face the bed.

'How you doing?' she said.

'Uh, fine? Shouldn't I be?'

She laughed, a bit too high, and pulled the chair closer. 'I just . . . wanted to check how you were. With Danny. And the guys at school. You know—'

I let out a groan. 'Jess, that's so sweet, really, but you don't need to.'

She bit her lip. 'I just hate the idea of those idiots getting to you. I know how hard school can be, and you know I'm not exactly Miss Popular, but it's great what you and Danny have, being mates, and it's not worth spoiling just because some spotty gits have noticed you're a girl.'

'Be fair,' I said, 'they're not all spotty. Philip, Scott, they're good-looking guys. I'd be lucky if they swept me off my feet.'

She swatted at my feet, safe under the covers. 'You know what I mean.'

She looked so serious, so earnest, I couldn't help but smile. It was amazing that she cared so much, that she'd fight for me, that she bothered at all.

'You're a good person,' I said, and her cheeks reddened a little. 'But you don't need to worry about Danny and me. Trust me. We're solid, and if the rugger buggers have an issue with that, I'll thump 'em myself.'

'There's my little sister,' said Jess, and she was beaming now. She ran her hand through her hair, catching a knot, pulling it out. I smelled her shampoo and pulled the duvet tighter.

'Good way to end the day,' I said.

'Mmm. How was school?'

I thought about the house, the smell of the sea, and the man, and running, fighting with him on Danny's bike, and my poor, broken bag.

'Interesting,' I said. Jess raised an eyebrow.

'Now I really am suspicious.' She stood up, put the chair back to its place, and moved towards the door. 'Don't have too many adventures without me,' she said. She pulled the door open and a wave of colder air slid against my arms.

'Jess . . . ' I said.

'Yeah?'

'Thanks. You're a . . . good egg.'

She looked pleased and tossed her hair dramatically. 'Anytime, darling. I'm always open for house calls. Mwah!'

She stepped out, closing the door in one smooth movement.

'Loser!' I shouted, and then she was gone.

A few moments later Dee was back, her head appearing through the curtains, her eyes, so large, so curious, watching me as she appeared.

'You didn't need to leave,' I said.

'I wanted to be . . . polite.'

137

'One of Death's better qualities, that,' I said. I grabbed my phone from the bedside table. 'Why hasn't Danny answered?'

'Do you want me to check on him?'

'Ha, no. No. He wouldn't like that. He doesn't *have* to answer, anyway.' I looked up at Dee, saw her face, the frown that crumpled her forehead. She was staring at the wall, or maybe beyond it, to Danny's room, to whatever he was doing.

'You shouldn't spy!' I said. Then, 'What's wrong?'

She looked like she was concentrating. 'Nothing,' she said. 'Just . . . no, nothing. You're right. I shouldn't spy.'

I put down my phone, turned off the light. As she moved to the window, Dee seemed to glow, a ghost-girl, a moon-girl watching through the darkness.

It was later – much later – that Danny texted back. *Soz,* he said. *Wasn't here. World Between. Didn't see message.*

'Without me,' I muttered, squinting at the brightness of the screen, already turning over, falling back to sleep, letting my mind wander. Beside me Dee was frowning again.

At school the next day it felt like Danny was avoiding me. I saw him just as the bell rang for registration, chatting with some guys I didn't know, and he looked tired and strange. Garth was standing nearby, looking out at the crush of kids and bags and teachers and noise, frozen to the spot by some odd fascination.

'Are we really that interesting?' I whispered to Dee. She looked at Garth, tutted, but she was smiling.

'Life is interesting,' she said. 'Especially to ... to us. We're used to seeing it one by one. Being here, it's a flood, a flood of light and sound and ... well, life.'

'You're used to matches,' I said, 'and now you're standing in a floodlit field.'

She beamed. 'Yes! Wonderful. *Like a floodlit field.* This language, I thought it was so imprecise, because things never mean what they look like, do they? But now I think it is better than that, wider. Things always means *more* that you say, they mean double, they layer up. Magic.'

'Ha, nerd,' I said, and she pulled a face.

We kept moving, weaving our way through the corridor, and I wondered if Danny had seen us, had looked for us at all.

'I hate myself sometimes,' I said. Dee looked surprised, stopping so suddenly she could have been frozen in time.

'Why do you say that?'

I laughed. 'No, not like that, not literally. I just mean ... I wish I didn't think certain things. I'm worried about Danny; I'm acting like some stupid cartoon princess. Next thing you know I'll be swooning and dropping handkerchiefs. If that happens, please do kill me. Take me with you to the Undying Lands or whatever it is you do.'

'I don't know about Undying Lands ... '

'Look, I'm joking, it's fine. Come on.'

I looked back anyway, but Danny was laughing, joking, jostling. I swore at myself and kept on walking.

Sometimes you get annoyed at someone, and it's not their fault, and it's not even fair, but that doesn't stop it from happening. It stews, like a teabag left in the dregs, and because they're not there to make things better, to defend themselves, you start to really believe all the negative things you list about them. I spent the whole morning feeling *off*, feeling annoyed at Danny for reasons I couldn't place, feeling annoyed at myself for being silly and needy, for being selfish about Dee, for being a coward, for being to blame. Things got worse the more I let them, and by the class before lunch – history, which I actually quite liked – I was glaring at the world through a dark, angry mist. Everything the others did annoyed me. Everything the teacher said seemed stupid, forced, contrived. I *liked* Miss Van Huss, but as she stood in front of the class, gesturing as she talked, I just wanted them all to stop.

'The Industrial Revolution,' said Van Huss, pointing to the whiteboard, 'can never be seen as an isolated event. It was the culmination of decades of advancement in almost every field at the time – technology, engineering, medicine, politics, justice, agriculture – and the military, of course. Britain's place in the world wasn't a happy accident. Power came from the subjugation of others – through war and invasion and, often, blind profiteering.'

She paused and looked at our faces. Most were blank. If it bothered her, she didn't show it.

'The Industrial Revolution meant the rise of the machine, and with it, the rise of the workers.'

'I almost remember that,' said Dee.

I turned my head slightly and kept my voice low. 'I didn't know you could remember.'

She looked like she was concentrating, focusing on some point I couldn't see, some slippery idea just beyond reach.

'It's not ... memory,' she said, 'just ... ideas. A feeling. We've always been there, waiting for you, helping you cross, and then—'

'Yes?'

She shook her head. I grunted. 'Secrets. Right. Well, if you remember anything that'll help me with this class, let me know, yeah?'

'Philippa, do you have something to share?'

Miss Van Huss had the slightest smile on her face. Everyone turned to look at me and I knew my cheeks were reddening.

'Um, no. Sorry, miss. Just trying to remember it all.'

'Hmm,' she said. One by one the kids looked away.

'It's going to be a long day,' I whispered.

'Every day is long when you're alive,' said Dee. I rolled my eyes and turned back to my books.

141

We met up with the boys at lunch. Without anyone saying so, we'd made the spot by the science labs our own. It felt tucked away, as private as you could get at school. Danny didn't say so, but I knew we'd be less likely to be seen by his mates. I knew I shouldn't care. I smiled as I walked up to him.

'How's Paul?' I asked.

'Uh, good,' said Danny. He looked like he was trying to work out if I was joking, making fun. 'Thinking of going to grab a burger after school. You should come.'

'Thanks,' I said. 'Maybe.'

Garth was grinning. He moved through the air lazily, feet dangling above the ground, 'Well, this is nice and awkward,' he said. Dee tutted. Danny chuckled.

'He's right. It is, and it shouldn't be. How you doing? You all right after yesterday?'

'I'm fine,' I said. 'I mean, it was scary, yeah, but we got away, and we're safe, aren't we?'

'Yeah, yeah. Absolutely.'

Sunlight was falling through the leaves of the trees as they flexed in the breeze. It flickered, like the reflections of a pool, on our faces, on the ground. Dee and Garth didn't have shadows. I'd never noticed that before.

'You were in the World Between,' I said. I didn't mean much by it – it was something to say, to keep us talking. Danny's face darkened and he stood perfectly still.

'Yeah, I was. I can go alone. Garth'll tell you, it's fine.'

I blinked. 'What? I didn't mean it was a problem. I was just saying. Why would you—'

'You've been without me,' he said. He pulled his phone from his pocket, glanced at the screen, shoved it back in.

'Well, yeah, sure.'

'So you know how ... how amazing it is.'

He sounded almost distant. Garth was watching him.

'It's like nowhere else I've been,' I said. 'The whole place buzzes, like it's made of electricity and life.'

His shoulders relaxed. 'Yeah!' he said. 'Life. That's it. It's better than a holiday, right? Better than ... than anything.'

We were both smiling again. I liked this. Garth was hovering, a dark, angry bird, but I ignored him. For a moment I could ignore everything, and pretend things were normal again, that everything wasn't changing faster than I wanted. I fiddled with the straps on my bag, listened to the sounds of the school, let my mind wander, back to the ocean, the way it sounded, the way it seasoned the world when you were near it.

'We should go again later,' said Danny.

'To the house?'

He looked at me like I was an idiot. 'No. You know where.'

I was still annoyed, but I wanted things to be fine, to stop being so much effort. 'Sure, we can. That's fine, right, Dee?'

She looked at Garth, almost too quick to notice. 'We should really work on finding the book ... ' she said.

'That place isn't just some game,' said Garth. I shrugged,

but Danny looked angry, biting his lip like he was trying to hold something in.

'I mean, I guess we could,' I said. 'It's not dangerous, right, Dee?'

She paused. 'No,' she said, 'but—'

'Come on, Phil, we went together, you know it's fine. Let's just do it – we could just head home now, or just find an empty classroom and—'

'Danny,' I said, and he grunted in frustration, stepping backwards.

'Fine! Fine. Just a thought. Fun thing to do, yeah?'

'No, I know, it's just – the book, you know, and we don't really have, like, a plan at all, and—'

'Fine,' he said again. 'Don't worry. Just chill, Phil. Sorry, *Philippa*.'

'I am chill.'

'Cool. Cool.'

Neither of us spoke. Danny was smiling, but there was something cold behind it. The wind picked up dust from the playground, sent it swirling and scattering. Danny looked down, kicked at a stone near his foot, and we both watched it skip and tap across the concrete, rolling towards the school gates. It hit a metal post with an echoing *ding* and came to a spinning stop. A group of kids was standing by inside the gate, and Ms Caçala, from the French department, was talking to a man just outside. The man looked past her, taking in the school and the playground, and as he turned his head our eyes met. He smiled, and for a second I thought of him as a fox, sharp toothed and lean, and then I backed away, tugging Danny's arm.

'That man!' I hissed, stepping back further behind the science block, out of view of the gate.

'No. No way.'

'It is, isn't it?'

'Bloody hell, Phil!'

'What?' said Garth. He floated up, rising higher and higher off the ground until his head was far above the buildings. I watched him like I was watching a show, and this strange thought – that he could fly, that it was as easy to him as walking – echoed in my head from far away.

'That man,' I said again. Then Dee understood, and she smiled, and she looked almost afraid.

'I guess we don't need to worry about finding them,' she said. 'Congratulations, Philippa. *They* found *you*.'

Danny swore under his breath, then louder, his cheeks getting paler.

'These people,' he said, then he shook his head. 'This is messed up.'

'How'd they find us?' I said, but even as I said it a new thought had blossomed in my mind, a horrible flower suddenly bursting into colour.

'My bag,' I said. 'The part he ripped. It had the school badge on. It might as well have been a bloody map.'

Danny ran his hands through his hair. 'He can't come

into school. People can't just walk into schools. We're safe here.'

'Right.'

'I mean, we are, right?'

I looked at Garth and Dee.

'They're not magicians,' said Dee. 'They're not going to do anything you couldn't.'

'Oh yeah,' said Danny, ''cause I try to summon Death all the time. Fun Friday night, that is.'

Garth rose up again, sailing over the roof of the science block and searching the road beyond the gate.

'He's gone,' he called down to us.

'He saw me. He definitely saw me,' I said.

'Then we need to face the fact that they'll come for you,' said Dee.

'Why? Because we messed things up?'

'Because you saw them,' she said. 'Because you know what they're doing.' She paused. 'What they've done.'

I shot Danny a look. 'Why'd you have to ... to goad him yesterday?'

'They already knew,' he said. 'It doesn't matter.'

'It does! It—'

'Philippa,' he said, and I stopped. 'It's us versus them. That's it. OK?'

'We have to tell someone,' I said. 'The police, or the teachers, or even a priest, I don't know!'

'Calm down, Phil!' Danny snapped. 'We can't ask for

146

help! What would you say? That a group with a magic book are after us because we broke into a house and saw them summoning the devil?' He laughed, a cold, sarcastic burst of sound. 'You do that, but don't drag me into it.'

'Don't tell me to calm down like I'm overreacting to this!'

'Well, don't be such a girl about it, shrieking and—'

I pushed him, not hard, but hard enough that he fell back against the wall, knocking the back of his head.

'Ow! What the hell?'

'Guys,' said Garth, 'please, we should—'

'You're such a prick sometimes, Danny,' I said. He rubbed his head, his eyes full of shock, then anger.

'You pushed me! You bloody pushed me!'

'Yeah, well, you're an idiot, acting like I'm—'

'You're a nutter sometimes, you know that?'

Now I laughed, turning away, trying to calm down, not wanting to.

'You're turning into such a jerk,' I said. 'Changing, all 'cause you want to be cool.'

His face was dark with anger. Garth and Dee watched us, frozen, glancing at each other for some clue as to what to say.

'If I wanted to be *cool*,' said Danny, 'then why would I be hanging out with you? God, you're so ... ridiculous some-times! I'm out of here.'

'I'm sure the rugger buggers are waiting!' I snapped. He glared at me, then turned and marched away through the crowd of kids and noise.

'I should . . . ' said Garth, his worlds trailing off into the breeze. He nodded once at Dee and followed Danny, hurrying to catch up. I looked down, wiping my eyes, wishing I wasn't so stupid, that things could be back to normal, that the world would just make sense for a bit.

EIGHT

B<small>Y LATE</small> afternoon my anger had fizzled away. I sat in Geography, doodling in the margins of my book, while Mr Allcock tried to make us care about magma flow. The sky had turned dark again, and thin drizzle coated the world. The school smelled of stale air, trapped energy, impatience. The air was too thick, the desks too close. I fidgeted and tried to pay attention.

'Why do you learn about this?' asked Dee. She didn't need to whisper – no one else could hear her – but I wished she would. I sighed and put down my pencil.

'We have to,' I said, as quietly as I could, trying not to move my lips.

Next to me, Suneeta Jindal raised her eyebrows. 'What?' she said. I felt my cheeks flush.

'Just . . . singing,' I said. The corners of her mouth flicked into a smile and I looked back down at my books. Dee was still listening to Mr Allcock.

'Why magma, though?' she said.

I held my hand up to cover my mouth. 'What do you mean?'

'Why do you need to learn about these things? They're so distant and . . . immense.'

I shrugged. I didn't know. She leaned forward and stared at the whiteboard.

'This is amazing,' she said. 'I never knew any of this.' I shifted away from Suneeta.

'If you want to take notes,' I said, 'be my guest.'

'If I could hold a pencil, maybe I would.'

I went back to doodling. It was a scribble of a boy, a sword sticking from his back, something horrendous happening to the rest of him.

'So it builds up for *years*,' Dee muttered, 'and then . . . poof! Eruption. Wow.'

I stopped doodling and smiled.

'When it leaves the earth, it's called lava, not magma,' I said. Suneeta was leaning away from me now, saying something to Gemma Cleaver. I hoped it wasn't about me.

'Why?' said Dee.

'Hmm?'

'Why is it lava, not magma?'

'No idea. Words are slippery, I guess.'

Gemma was laughing. I stared down at my page. Drops of rain – proper fat ones that popped and pinged off the glass – turned the world outside into a noisy, colourless mess. I didn't have an umbrella. Walking home would be a pain.

'Garth!' said Dee, shouting and jumping up. I flinched, knocking my pencil case to the floor, scattering what was inside. A few of the kids turned and glanced at me, looked away again. Mr Allcock smiled and straightened his glasses.

'Everything all right, Miss Ravenhurst?'

I bent down, picked up my stuff, tried to ignore Dee's muffled laughter. 'Dropped something,' I said, looking over to the door where Garth had appeared, moving through it like it was nothing. He looked a little sorry, at least.

'Very well. Settle down, guys. Just twenty minutes left, I promise. So, what we have here ... '

Garth sat down beside me. Dee stood next to him, silent, unreadable. I tilted my head and waited.

'Message from Danny,' he said.

He's sorry? I mouthed. I leaned on my hand, facing the wall. No one seemed to notice.

'Not exactly,' said Garth. He looked awkward. I didn't care.

'He knows he should be, right?' I whispered.

'He's confused by how that all happened, I think.'

I snorted, turned it into a cough. 'Oh, poor thing.'

'Philippa,' said Dee, 'we have to focus on bigger things.'

I pushed the nib of my pencil into the paper until it snapped off and crumbled into peppery dust.

'Fine,' I said.

'Danny's message,' said Garth. 'Can I give it?'

'Better than a text, you are.'

If he was bothered by that, he didn't show it. He smiled weakly and leaned forward.

'They know we're here and we have to get ready. You should meet up before leaving the school. It might even be best to go out the back, try jumping over the fence across the playing field. He doesn't want to split up and give them a chance to find you.'

'Makes sense.'

'So will you meet him by the library stairs right after this?'

Even if I didn't want to, what he was saying made sense. I nodded, brushing the bits of lead from my book onto the floor. Garth stood up, whispered something to Dee, and headed back out the room, nothing more than the shadow of a ghost.

'Neat trick,' I said.

'Spectres,' said Dee, her voice light and casual. 'Cheaper than e-mail, rubbish at holding stuff.'

Despite everything, I smiled, and I could see that made Dee happy. The rain outside was getting worse, but the clock kept moving, and school would be over soon enough. Next to me, Suneeta leaned closer.

'You talk to yourself. You know that?'

Kids pushed past me, jostling each other to get to the bus, get to their parents, get out of school. The air was buzzing with chatter and laughter. Dee floated above it all, a curious look on her face, like a scientist observing a misbehaving insect. The library stairs were on the other side of the school to the geography classrooms, but even going against the crowd, we were only a few minutes away.

'Wait up!' someone called, and I smelled perfume, and sharp, fake cheese, and teenage boys wearing too much deodorant. I pushed myself against the wall as a flutter of Year Sevens ran by, and then Jess was by my side, her blazer spotted with raindrops. She was catching her breath and strands of hair were stuck to her cheek.

'What a zoo!' she said.

'It's a grey day. It's like letting all the prisoners out.'

'Want to call Mum and see if she can pick us up?'

'Oh. No, I'm not heading home straight away. I just have to ... do a thing.'

Idiot, I thought. Any lie – anything – would have been better than that.

'Do a thing? Do tell.'

'No, it's nothing special, I just ... I'm just meeting Danny and hanging out.'

Jess made a weird face, like she was trying to decide if I was joking, or if she should make a joke.

'And what will you be doing? Should I be worried?'

'Jess,' I said. 'Not now.' Another group of boys ran past, their shoes caked in shining mud.

'Well, fine. I won't stay up.'

153

'Jess.'

'I'm just teasing, Pip.'

Pip. That was a new one.

'We're just sorting something out. It's fine.'

'It's a good thing you're such an accomplished liar,' she said, 'or I'd be pretty damn curious about all this.'

With that she melted away back into the crowd, waving as she did so.

'Come on,' said Dee, who'd watched from above, unseen, unheard. 'We should hurry while there are still so many people about as a distraction.'

I joined the rush again, jostling the other students, my mind racing. How had it got to this – to trying to *escape* the school? It felt like a terrible movie. Dee floated above, those green eyes staring down at the mass of kids and bags and shouts, and I wanted to laugh, or shout out and tell them how big the universe was, how much they didn't know ...

'There,' said Dee brightly. The library was coming up on the left, and standing just inside the stairs up to the doors, Danny was leaning against the wall, eyes moving from face to face. When he saw me, he relaxed, straightened up, called me over.

'You got the message,' he said.

'Yup. Ghost Express.'

'We're not ghosts,' said Garth, but he didn't sound annoyed enough to argue. Danny ran his hand through his hair, messing it up. I tried to look patient, uninterested.

'We should probably get going,' he said.

'While there's crowds. OK.'

'If we go out the back it makes sense, right?'

'Sure. I mean, if they're watching the front, and they want to catch us, yeah.'

'Cool. Cool.'

'These guys are so on the ball,' said Garth, stage-whispering to Dee behind a cupped hand. 'It's impressive.'

'Shut up, man,' said Danny, but he smiled a little, and so did I.

'This is so weird, right?' I said.

'It's not what I'd been planning to do, no.'

'Should we warn anyone?'

'I don't know. I mean, are they dangerous? To other people?'

'Anyone can be dangerous,' said Dee. She sighed. 'But no, right now, I don't think they're a threat to anyone but you two. They want to know who you are, what you saw.'

'Shouldn't we try to talk to them, get the book back?' said Danny.

'No way,' I said. 'Not here. They have us totally out-matched. We're not ready for a ... a fight, or whatever.'

He knew I was right, but he was wound up, scared, itching to do something.

'She's right,' said Garth. 'What would you do right here? People could get hurt. Now we know we don't have to find them, we can make a plan – a good plan – when we're home safe. Yeah?'

It was three against one, and Danny knew it. He scratched his face. 'Sure. Whatever. We should go then. Come on.'

We moved through the hallways, the crowds already thinning as the school emptied and echoed with the quiet. Groups were still dotted around, huddled together, gossiping, chatting, laughing, and I felt a pang of envy for something so normal and nice. It seemed a million miles away now, like some other world I might never get to see. We carried on, turning right, turning left, pushing through doors, going over a concrete quad and back into the modern-languages block, out again, and then the field was there in front of us, wet and muddy and cold.

'Amazing we don't come out this way more often,' I said.

'Some of the guys do after practice. There's a chippie you can get to if you just jump over the bit by those trees. I've been a few times.'

'Oh.'

Why did that annoy me? I didn't want it to, but it was another glimpse at a life I didn't know, one I wasn't part of. I tried to sound casual.

'Maybe I'll come some time.'

'Uh, yeah. Maybe. Come on.'

We started crossing the field, Danny waving at a few boys kicking a ball back and forth, trying to hear what they shouted at him. The sound was swallowed by the wind and he just waved again, grinning.

'So many admirers,' I said. He ignored me, but his smile

faded a little. I shouldn't have said anything, but I was glad I had. I hid my smirk.

'There,' said Danny, pointing forward to a row of thin hedges gasping for life in front of a chain-link fence. 'If we get over that, it's easy, and I bet no one'll see us.'

'Not from the school?'

'They'd have to be looking right here, and if they are, then we're already screwed, right?'

'I guess.'

I looked up. The clouds were getting darker again, a thick white shadow pregnant with storms. I didn't have an umbrella. Mum would kill me if I soaked my school blazer. The wind – not too bad right now, but a weak sting on my cheeks – was thick with the smells of cars and oil and the town. We kept walking, getting faster – nervous, I think – and then we were there, and I could see the road on the other side, the houses and shops beyond it, the town spreading out beyond the school.

'I've never been on this side,' I said, more to myself than anyone. 'How can I come here for, like, years and never know where this road goes?'

Nobody answered. Danny slung his bag off his shoulder and tossed it over the fence. It landed with a crunch on the pavement. He winced.

'There go the glasses I stole from chemistry!'

'Lame,' I told him. I watched as he climbed up the fence, using the wire holes to get his feet in, pulling himself up and over, and falling back down with a satisfying *crack* of shoes on pavement.

'Your turn,' he said.

He looked through the fence at me and spread his arms open.

'Need a hand?'

'As if.' I eyed the fence, pulled off my bag and swung it back.

'Catch.'

The bag sailed through the air, up and over the fence and down into Danny's arms.

'Oof!' he said as it hit his chest. 'Man, what you got in here?'

'Oh, heads of my enemies, secret girl stuff, y'know, the usual.'

He put the bag down and folded his arms.

'This I got to see.'

I looked at Dee and rolled my eyes. 'He thinks he's Mr Athletic.'

She smiled but said nothing, floating up and over the fence, landing down next to Danny without a sound. He looked at her and I thought he looked a little less pleased, but then he turned back to me.

'Any day now. This is meant to be a speedy, secret escape, you know.'

'Oh, for goodness' sake.'

I grabbed the fence, pulling myself up and pushing

the tips of my shoes into the wire holes. At the top the whole thing swayed, but it was easily strong enough, and I gripped tightly as I swung my legs over and started climbing down, dropping when I was a couple of feet off the ground.

'Wonder Woman,' said Danny.

'That was nothing special, dickweed.'

'Hey!'

'What's wrong, Superman?'

I picked up my bag and pulled it tight on my shoulders.

'So, this way?' I said, starting down the road.

'Yeah. Yeah, we can swing round, and then head down towards the old swimming pool, then back home along the cliffs.'

'Great.'

'We should stay in busy places,' said Garth. 'The cliff path, it seems exposed.'

'But no one really goes there,' said Danny.

'We thought that about the house, though,' I said. He looked annoyed.

'*You* thought that about the house. I would never even have gone in!'

'Like I knew all this would happen? It was just bad luck we were there when those freaks turned up!'

The air was crackling with a brewing fight again. We both knew it, and we stood our ground, holding our tongues, hoping the other would break first.

'If you hadn't been there,' said Dee, 'the Society would have succeeded. It's a blessing for the world that you were.'

'Regular heroes, we are,' said Danny. He sounded bitter again, sullen and stupid.

'Whatever. Let's get home.'

He nodded and pulled his school tie loose. 'OK. This way.'

We started walking. I looked across the road at the row of shops I'd never really known about. Vegetables lay in crates, newspapers tucked into stands, snacks and clothes and jewellery all on sale, all on offer. It was all so close to school, but I felt like I was so far from home. A couple of kids were walking towards us, guys from the year below who must have gone out the proper way and walked around to get here. So many lives, so many different things – and none of them knew what we were doing, what we'd got ourselves into. Garth and Dee were silent, walking alongside us, their eyes taking in everything. I wondered how mad I'd look talking to Dee, if it would look like I was talking to Danny. Maybe no one would care.

'Round here,' said Danny, nodding to the corner ahead. 'We cross the road and we can take the long way, see?'

'Great.'

'Great. Let's cross.'

We'd reached a crossroad, four different roads that snaked off away from each other. The left, I guessed, would take us back to the school – it must have been where the other kids came from. Going straight would probably take us home, eventually, but I couldn't say for certain. Going right seemed even stranger, but if we were trying to stay safe, Danny's idea made sense. We reached the corner and waited for the lights to change.

'So,' said Danny, 'how was your day?'

'Um, fine. Boring. Geography with Mr Allcock.'

Danny groaned. 'Oh, man, I had him last year. Does he still make that joke about sitting on the fence?'

'Oh, yeah. "You're going to get a sore bum, Philippa! Now give me a straight answer." Ew.'

'Ah, he's not a creep, just a bit lame.'

'Definitely lame. Maybe funny the first time. Never after that.'

'Ha, for sure.'

The lights were changing, the cars slowing down.

'All right, let's go,' said Danny, and even as he said it I felt a hand, thin and firm, grab my shoulder and pull me away from the kerb. I jumped in surprise, saw Danny being pulled back, turned around and stopped. A woman was standing right behind us, her hands clamped down on our shoulders, a cold, calm smile frozen on her face.

'Here you are, my lovelies,' she said. 'We almost didn't find you! Sneaking out? Is that it?'

The traffic light was beeping behind us, but it sounded like it was so far away. I tried to say something, felt my throat tighten, my mind blank. Danny jerked himself away, reaching up and grabbing her wrist.

'Get off!' he shouted. 'Get off me!'

The woman's smile was plastic perfect. 'If you make any fuss, we will deal with your families. Don't make things worse for yourself.'

'You can't—'

She slapped him, not hard, but casually across the face, her eyes darting up to see if anyone had seen, if any cars would stop. Danny's eyes went wide and he reached out for me.

'Your families,' the woman said again. 'I mean it. Don't cause such a scene.'

'We're not—' I said, but her fingers pinched into my shoulder and she leaned forward until her face was only inches from mine.

'Don't test me. You've no idea what you've stumbled into.'

She pulled again, dragging us away from the road and down the street.

'Think you're so clever,' she muttered, 'going out the back, as if we wouldn't think of that. Come on, you idiot.'

She jerked Danny forward again. He looked scared, eyes wild, not sure what to do, his feet stumbling as the woman kept pulling us forward.

'Don't go with her!' said Dee. She was next to me suddenly, speaking urgently, her eyes bright and shining. 'Just pull away, run!'

'My family . . .' I said. This was a bad dream, a daze, something I was watching from far, far away . . .

'Forget that, just run!' shouted Garth. Danny looked at

him, confused, tried to come to a stop. The woman turned back to him and scoffed.

'Maybe I could tell your school what you've been up to?' she said. 'Trespassing, vandalism, and then trying to mug me! I have witnesses, you know. We'll all swear you stole my handbag.'

'She's making it up!' said Garth. 'You see that?'

'But—' said Danny, and she slapped him again, a sudden, cat-like flick, and then her hand was back on his shoulder.

'No!' I shouted.

'You want one too?' she said.

My eyes were watering, my whole body numb with shock. I looked at Dee.

'Help, please,' I said. 'Do something!'

'Your boyfriend won't help you now,' said the woman.

'Dee, please, you have to be able to—'

'I said your boyfriend's no use!' said the woman. 'And what are you looking at? What is this?'

'Please,' I said again. The woman laughed and shook her head. 'Off your head on drugs,' she said. 'Doing drugs and mugging women. Oh, kids today.'

'Do something!' I shouted, a burst of noise and fear that echoed in the street.

'Garth!' said Dee, and her eyes widened. I span, and as I did the woman's grip fell away, her arms falling limp by her side. I stumbled back, looked up, and gasped. Garth was floating behind the woman, his face twisted with effort, his eyes shut tight. His hands were pressed on the sides of the woman's face, but his fingers – I looked away, looked back, felt sick – were buried up to the knuckle in her head. Thin rays of light flashed where his fingers met the skin, and the woman stood rigid, her eyes empty and staring, her head lolling slightly.

'What the f—' started Danny, and he stared in horror as Garth's eyes moved under their lids.

'He's . . . he's helping,' said Dee.

'His fingers are in her brain!'

'It was the only way. She's strong, she was dangerous, he had to go deep . . .'

'Oh my God,' said Danny. He rubbed his face, breathing deeply. 'Oh my God, oh my God.'

'But what is this?' I said.

Dee looked serious. 'If you thought what I did to Paul was bad . . .'

The woman gasped, making us all jump. Slowly, impossibly, Garth's fingers slid out of her head, leaving no marks, no blood, no scars. She let out a juddering sigh and fell against the brick wall. Garth's eyes flickered, opened, and he shook his hands as if they were wet.

'That was dangerous,' said Dee.

'She won't remember any of this. I made sure.'

Dee chewed her lip. 'Really?'

'Really.'

'You were careful?'

'She won't remember.'

He looked down at the ground, let his eyes rise up to the woman still leaning nearby, her face blank, her mouth hanging open.

'You destroyed her,' said Dee.

I blinked, the words not making sense. 'What?'

'I went too deep,' said Garth. 'I wanted to find answers.'

'You took?' said Dee.

'I found what we need. I know where the book is.'

'But what have you done to her?' I said.

'I – I didn't mean to,' said Garth. 'I panicked. You were shouting, and we had no time, and I . . . I thought—'

He stopped, his chest moving as he breathed in and out. Danny moved towards the woman. She smiled at him, her eyes barely focusing, and then she looked away at the sky, at nothing.

'She's alive,' he said. 'Good. Come on. We have to go.'

'We can't just leave her!'

'Why not? They'll find her. Someone will. We have to go.'

'But – but this isn't—'

'Philippa!'

He looked surprised that he'd shouted at me, but he pressed forward. 'Come on. Let's go.'

I looked at the others, at the woman still staring at the clouds.

'You know where the book is?' Danny asked Garth.

'She knew. Now I do.'

He moved closer to the woman, raising a hand and almost touching her cheek. 'I'm sorry,' he said.

'Bubbles,' said the woman. 'Bubbles in the sky.'

I felt sick. I looked away.

'We should still take the cliff path,' said Danny. 'If she was here, there'll be more. Phil, stop wasting time! Let's go!'

Without another word, we ran, back down the street, though the lights, and away from the school, from the danger, from the woman.

NINE

As soon as I could smell the salt, hear the hiss of the waves, I stopped. We'd been running, getting faster as panic poisoned our minds, until I'd called out to Danny to slow down, to not leave me behind. Roads turned to alleyways, turned to fields and paths, and now we faced the edge of the world, and just the grey water beyond.

'We're not being followed,' said Dee. 'I've been checking. There's no way.'

The wind was wild here. My hair spilled around my face. I breathed in, breathed out. Garth was whispering with Danny, looking over at me, turning away.

'Are you all right?'

Dee was calm and quiet now.

'What did we do? What did Garth do?'

'What he had to do, I think. She was trying to kidnap you, Philippa.'

'But – we could have got away.'

'We did get away.'

Breathe in, breathe out. The smell of the sea all around.

'It's beautiful,' said Dee. I sniffed. My whole body felt numb.

'What? Yeah. Like your world between worlds,' I said.

'Hmm? That's different,' said Dee. 'That place isn't as real as this.'

'It felt pretty damn real.'

'It's a dead end. Believe me.'

I looked up at the clouds above the water. 'Other worlds,' I said. 'I can't believe I even say stuff like that. Other worlds. Spectres. Death and a magic book.'

'Book of magic,' said Dee. 'It's a normal book, apart from what's in it.'

The grass crunched behind us. Danny and Garth stood awkwardly nearby.

'You OK?' said Danny.

'Oh, just peachy.'

'The book—' he began.

'Not now. Please. Just . . . wait.'

'But these guys,' said Danny, spreading his hands out to take in Dee and Garth, 'they need to get home, the book is their way, and—'

'We're not doing anything tonight, though, are we? No, don't try to answer, I'm telling you, we can't! There's – there's homework, and Mum and Dad are probably already wondering where I am. There's normal life to do, OK?'

'But—'

'Don't you have practice?'

His face darkened. 'I thought this was more important,' he said.

'So some things are more important than rugby, that's good to know.'

It was a stupid thing to say – a low blow, and I knew it. I was being whiney and dumb, but I was scared now, and that woman had attacked us, hadn't she? Danny picked at his lip and scuffed his shoes in the sandy clay.

'I didn't know these people were actually dangerous,' he said.

'Huh?'

'Like, it all seemed like a game, didn't it? But then she grabbed you, and she was going to hurt you, and I wanted to kill her, but she was saying those things, and I swear, Phil, if she'd hit you I would have snapped, I would, I wouldn't have cared about school or Mum and Dad or anything, I'd have screamed and kicked, you know I would . . . '

I could hear seagulls somewhere below us, their screams snatched up by the gusts of wind and spray. Danny's breathing was heavy, his face more serious than I'd ever seen it.

'It's not a game,' I said.

'No. Maybe we should drop it. Talk about this later. Go home, make sure we're OK. That's cool, right, Garth?'

Garth was a dark shape against the light that spilled over the cliffs. His eyes were the same colour as the sky behind him, making him looking hollow when he looked at me.

'We can wait. You didn't ask for this. Things will be easier now anyway. Right, Dee?'

Dee nodded. 'You've both been ... awesome. Garth's right – you didn't ask for this. We can wait another day.'

'Tomorrow,' I said, feeling guilty. 'I promise. We can skip school. It's probably safer anyway. Tomorrow we'll get the book. Tomorrow we'll send you home.'

Dee beamed. 'You're not half bad, you humans.'

'Uh, thanks. That means a lot coming from a Deathling.'

'Deathling!' She laughed, and her eyes flashed with pale green fire.

'Better than spectre,' said Garth.

I looked out at the sea again, then back towards Danny. He had a strange look on his face – fear, anger, something like panic. He swallowed, saw me watching, and grinned with a big thumbs-up.

'I,' he said, 'am freezing my balls off.'

'Thanks for sharing.'

'Well, it's true. Let's head home. I'm worried about them, really I am.'

Garth chuckled and Dee rolled her eyes. The seagulls called out and we set off along the path snaking its way back towards town.

I pulled the curtains closed, glancing just once at the slit of a moon that hung above us. We were in my room now, safe and secure. We'd had lasagne for dinner, and it had been normal and nice. I ran my hands through my hair and stretched my neck from side to side.

'You did better not looking right at me,' said Dee. 'With your family around, I mean.' She was sitting on the bed, hands in her lap.

'Fast learner, me. It must have been boring for you, though.'

'I like your family. I like watching you all.'

'Little bit creepy, that.'

'Oh.'

I could hear Jess in the shower. Mum and Dad were laughing about something downstairs. I pulled my phone from my pocket and typed out a message: *Hey, you OK?*

Five minutes passed. No answer.

'He couldn't be asleep,' I said.

'Hmm?'

'Danny, he didn't reply to my text.'

'Are you worried?'

The shower had stopped. I closed the door to my room and lowered my voice.

'I just wanted to check. Today has been . . . ' I trailed off. 'It makes sense to check,' I said.

'I can check if you want. This wall goes straight into his house.'

She turned to the wall above my bed, waving her hand towards it. 'Nothing but air, really.'

I thought about it. 'That's a little bit creepy. No, actually, it's a lot creepy. If Garth does that to me he's in for trouble.'

'You're sure?'

'No spying! Not right now. Danny doesn't have to text me back anyway. It's fine.'

She sat down on the bed again, humming something under her breath. I turned away so she couldn't see and typed as fast as I could.

Hey sleepyhead, we have plans to make.

I wondered if I should call him, told myself I was being stupid. I pulled back the curtain and peeked out onto the street. Electric light turned the world soft acid orange. The hum and splutter of a motorbike rolled through the air.

'I doubt they have any way of finding you here,' said Dee.

'They found us at school.'

'They found the school – hardly impressive – and then got lucky and saw you.'

She wanted to make me feel better, but all I could think about was that woman, how she looked, what they might think when they found her, if they found her ...

'How can you and Garth do those things?'

Dee didn't even look up.

'It's natural,' she said, then added, 'For us.'

'But you're just parts of something, aren't you? You said that when things went wrong, you got cut off here, you were just the first, I don't know, tendrils poking through.'

'Not everything in the world is as simple as people.'

'People aren't simple,' I said.

'Hmm.'

'What?'

'I don't know how to explain it. We're from a different place. We're individual, we're all one. Death is a force that has endless potential. That's why the idea that humans could trap us, could command us – it's wrong. Worse. Evil.'

'I thought Death was evil.'

Now she did look up, and she looked almost shocked. 'Why?'

'You take people away!'

I was raising my voice. I made myself calm down.

'Death doesn't take people away. It – we – are just part of the world, we . . . we help guide, we make things work.'

It was too big to understand, too much to make sense of. I looked at Dee, at this girl, this strange, distant kid, and I tried to match what she was saying. I took a deep breath.

'So what happens . . . after?'

Dee narrowed her eyes, not suspicious, but wary.

'That's not something you need to worry about. You already know so much more than most. There are others places. The World Between showed you that.'

Even as she said it, I smelled the spice-wind, felt the warmth of moonlight on my face, felt the flames of those stars, so real, so solid and eternal.

'Knowing what's out there doesn't always mean good

173

things,' said Dee. 'Look at this … this Society. They're taking a little knowledge and making a huge mess.'

In that moment I felt small and pointless, a speck of dust facing the sun, a kid given a glimpse of how big the world could be.

'Danny isn't replying,' I said. I picked up my phone, unlocked the screen, turned it off again, threw it down on the bed.

'Busy day,' said Dee.

'Yeah.'

Someone in a house down the street was taking out their bins. I heard the clang of metal and glass, the thud of plastic being scraped along gravel.

'You can sleep,' said Dee. She leapt off the bed and landed silently, gracefully, on the carpet, moving too slowly for it to seem natural. 'I'll watch out. I'll check the street, it's fine.'

'My own invisible ghost guard.'

She wrinkled her nose at those words, but she did a fake little curtsey, too.

'Ghosts are a different thing.'

Was she joking? I couldn't tell.

'You sleep, Philippa. I'm going to see what happens on this street when the world turns dark.'

'Good luck with that. I think the answer is: nothing happens.'

She looked almost pitying, moving across the room to

stand near the window, her leg raised as if she could climb through it.

'Do you really think that?'

Before I could answer, she was gone, vanished through the wall and into the night. I pulled the curtains tight again and sat down, angry, annoyed, confused more than ever. I grabbed my phone and texted Danny.

You're a terrible person. Goodnight, sleeping beauty.

I waited a few minutes more, and when he didn't answer I pounded on the wall, as if he could hear me, then turned off my light and stared at the ceiling, willing sleep to come.

The dream was wild and angry, a storm of salt-spray and collapsing mountains. Wind rushed and waves pounded, pounded, pounded the boat. Someone screamed and I knew I had to hold on, pull the coarse rope between my hands, make something work or we'd all be crushed. Was there lightning? I think so. It was a dream, fuzzy-edged and too quick to pin down, but the roar was constant, the terror of the boat giving way under the storm. We would not drown – I knew that absolutely – but we would be crushed by the weight of the water and the foam. I shouted and swore and tried to steer towards land, and my eyes caught the flash of a lighthouse, or a candle in a window.

'There, there, row!' I screamed. The crew, which was bigger now, grabbed oars and rope and paddles, and we heaved and turned and begged the sodden wood to groan and change its course.

'We have to find shelter!'

Who was talking? I looked back, shielding my eyes, my lips cracking, my clothes sodden.

'The shore!' I shouted. 'The shore!'

But they shook their heads, eyes filled with fear, and I saw a flash reflected in them, the white-caps of waves as they split on razor rocks.

'Jump! Jump to the water!' they shouted, but I would not, it was insane, it was death, and I clung to the boat, the raw wood splintering in my palms, and it was damp, and it was melting like paper, and I fell and tasted water and bile and nothing else.

I woke up, aching and bleary-eyed, and Jess was in my room.

'Man, you're still in bed!' she said. 'Didn't your alarm go off? We have to leave in, like, half an hour.'

I blinked. I hid my eyes from the light. 'What?'

'Um, school? Education and learning and being normal. You know?'

I sat up, the echoes of waves rolling through my head. Dee was sitting at the desk near the window, watching Jess with patient curiosity.

'Why didn't you wake me up?' I asked her.

'What do you think this is?' said Jess. She followed my

eyes, looked around the room, waved at me. 'Right here, Your Majesty. Shall I avert my eyes while you de-bed?'

'You were sleeping quite soundly,' said Dee. 'I didn't know if I should—'

'OK, I'm up, I'm up. What time is it?'

'Time to get ready and go!' said Jess. 'I'll leave without you. Try to be on time, yeah?'

'Can Mum—'

'Already out. You're lucky, or she'd go mental at you. Maybe I should tell her—'

'I'm up,' I said again, pushing the duvet back and swinging my legs off the bed. 'All right? So just . . . leave me.'

Jess bowed solemnly and left the room backwards, keeping her eyes on the floor.

'I like her,' said Dee. 'She's respectful, isn't she?'

'She's a pain. Urgh, I need to shower. Wait there.'

I dragged myself into the shower, the water – too cold, too sharp – turning my skin to goose bumps, but waking me up. I changed the temperature and let the steam wrap around me. It didn't matter if I was late – in fact, this was better. I wasn't going to school. We had things to do.

Twenty minutes later I poked my head into Jess's room and gave her a quick wave. 'You go on,' I said. 'There's no way I'm going to be done. I'll just be late.'

She raised her eyebrows, then sighed. 'OK, but you're

telling Mum, and when you do, I put up a huge argument and practically tried to drag you out of here, right?'

'You are a virtuous warrior against my slovenly ways.'

'Damn right I am. Feel OK?'

'After my epic sleep, I feel better than ever. But, late. So . . .'

'Well,' she said, taking a bite of something on her desk, 'I'll see you later, then.'

'Got it.'

I didn't like lying to Jess, but there was no other way to get rid of her. Anything else, anything to raise her suspicions, would have made her stay here longer. Acting normal was the best lie of all. It worried me a little how easily it had come.

Back in my bedroom I got dressed and double-checked my phone.

'Good night?' I asked without looking up.

'Full of exploration. There's a family of foxes three houses down, did you know?'

'No,' I chuckled, 'I didn't.'

'Five kinds of birds, plus more snails than you could eat.'

'Ew.'

'Three cats, but only two that seem welcome, and a dog called Broccoli.'

'That's Mrs Davies' dog, I know him.'

'He's clever,' said Dee, 'but he's worried about her. She's going to be sick quite soon. She doesn't know yet.'

I stiffened a little, not taking my eyes off the shoes I was pulling on.

'Oh, and also, three rabbits and a hamster.'

'No mysterious people, then?'

'No.'

I took in a deep breath, stretched my fingers back. 'Good. Heard from Garth?'

Her face flickered, a moment of doubt she couldn't hide from me.

'I . . . haven't seen him, no. I called to him but didn't get an answer. I didn't go and look out of . . . respect. Should I try again?'

I shook my head. 'No. We'll knock, OK? Come on.'

I finished getting dressed and headed downstairs, calling out to make sure no one was home.

'Jess left,' said Dee. 'There's no one else here.'

'Good. Man, this is crazy! I've never just . . . not gone to school before.'

'Bad influence, me,' said Dee.

'Bad something,' I muttered. I grabbed my keys, pulled open the front door, double-checked I had my phone. Danny's dad's car was gone, so I guessed he was home alone, too – though I wondered how he'd got away with it. Would faking sickness work? His mum had always been too clever for that.

'Hey, Garth!' Dee shouted, cupping her hands around her mouth and craning her neck to look up at Danny's window. 'Hey!'

The curtains were closed. Nobody answered.

'Maybe he's in the shower,' I said.

'Both of them?' Dee smiled and winked. 'Hey hey,' she said.

'Who knows what these guys get up to,' I said, 'but I don't think that. Weird, though . . .'

I knocked on the door, rang the bell, knocked again. I tapped the wood, knocked more gently on the glass.

'He's definitely in, right?'

I bit my lip. He wouldn't have gone to school, not after last night, not without telling me or asking me to come. Maybe something was wrong.

'You know what?' I said. 'Go in. Check. We have to.'

'Really?'

'What else can we do? Just make sure he's not, like, lying at the bottom of the stairs or something. Let me know.'

I wished I hadn't said that. My mind filled with bloody images – Danny with his neck broken, his eyes hollow and staring. Danny sick with something, too weak to move, rasping in bed, trying to call out.

'Hurry,' I said, and Dee nodded once as she sprung up, rising quickly, stopping level with the window. In a heartbeat she passed through it, nothing more than light and smoke, and then she was gone, silent, hidden. I felt weirdly alone, then, like I shouldn't be here on the street at this time, staring at the house, with no excuse if someone came back, if someone saw. I fiddled with my hair, wondering if anyone was watching.

'Hey,' said Dee, and I jumped, turning just in time to see

her land back beside me. Her face was grim, her voice calm and hard as stone.

'What? What?'

'You have to come in.'

'What is it?'

'Come see!'

'How? He's— Oh, wait!'

I rushed back into my house, flinging the front door open as soon as I had the key in the lock. Where would it be? I knew they had one. I ran into the living room, to the desk in the corner covered in paper and bills and memories. I opened the top drawer, heard the clink of metal and plastic, and there it was – a string of keys: to the shed outside, to the locked filing cabinet, and there, dull gold and thick-headed, a key to Danny's house. This was for emergencies, or if someone got locked out, but this was an emergency, wasn't it? I ran back outside, the keys cold in my hand, and Dee was standing beside the front door.

'He's not dead,' she said. 'I should have said. But he needs us.'

'Us?'

I wasn't even listening. I focused on the key, getting it in the right way, turning it, hearing the click of the lock. I ran in, my mind filled with visions of what I might see, what had rattled Dee, what Danny might have done.

'Danny!' I shouted as I launched up the stairs. 'Danny! Hey! It's me!'

His bedroom door was shut. I stopped in front of us, knocking quickly, and I pushed the door open without waiting for an answer. Dee was behind me – I knew it, could feel it – and she spoke softly and pointed. 'Look. See.'

The room was no bigger than mine. I didn't need her to point out where he was. Danny was sitting on the edge of his bed, naked except for his boxers, his back ruler-straight, his eyes staring forward at the wall. I stepped closer, knelt down in front of him.

'What the hell?' I said. 'His eyes! Dee, what—'

'He's *there*,' she said. 'Garth is too. This is what you look like if you visit the World Between. But his eyes, yes. That doesn't seem right.'

Danny's eyes were open. A grey mist seemed to fill them, turning the whites, the pupils, everything into one sickly cloud. He wasn't blinking. He wasn't moving. I touched his arm, gripped his shoulder, tried to move him.

'Hey,' I said, then louder again, 'Oi, idiot, what are you doing? Come back!'

'He shouldn't be this deep,' said Dee, staring into his eyes, moving her hand to almost brush his face. 'And Garth, too. What are they doing?'

It felt weird being so close to Danny like this, like we'd walked in on something private. I made sure I didn't look down.

'This isn't good,' said Dee. She was muttering under her breath, counting, working something out.

'How long do you think he's been doing this?'

'I don't know,' I said.

'We have to go after them.'

'Go after them?' I laughed. 'You make it sound like a chase.'

'Look at him!' said Dee. 'Does he look OK? Humans aren't built to ... to go hopping around other places.'

'But you took me there!'

'For a short time, to show you, to prove what we said – it was Garth's idea, you know, to get Danny to understand.'

'Well, what do we do now?'

Dee looked at Danny, eyes bright, jaw set.

'I need you to hold his hand.'

'Um ... '

'So we can find them when we get there. Contact. That's all.'

I looked at Danny again. His boxers had the batman logo around the edge. His chest was moving in and out slowly, his breathing almost mechanical, and his eyes, grey, full of shadows ...

'Right. OK. God, I hope no one else comes home, if they see this—'

'It'll be fun,' said Dee. I reached down and took Danny's hand off the bed, forcing his arm up so I could wrap my fingers around his. His skin was cold, his muscles tense.

'Ready?' said Dee.

'Danny,' I whispered, 'we're coming, OK?'

'That's a yes,' said Dee, and with a rush of sound and wind and light, we left the room, and the house, and the world.

TEN

DAWN WAS coming in the World Between. Streaks of pink light coiled through the sky, shredding the velvet, licking the stars. We were among the trees, among their creaks and groans. The earth was black and covered with moss. The air smelled of wood here, and smoke and chocolate. My skin prickled.

'Danny should be close,' said Dee. She looked up at the stars and smiled.

'I do like it here,' she said. 'I'll have to see if I can come back, once we're home.'

'I love it here,' I said. I put my hand on the nearest trunk – the bark crumbled, frail as dust, but the tree was huge and eternal. It thrummed with life, like a pulse, an eternal sway. Dee said nothing. She floated up and closed her eyes.

'Garth,' she said, and she cocked her head. 'Yes. Here. Here, this way.'

She moved quickly, and I had to call after her, break

into a run, to even keep up. We darted left, right, left again, through clumps of bushes, into puddles that threw out pale silver light, into a clearing that rolled with lavender and honeysuckle, back into the shadows of the woods, darting, pushing, running.

'Here,' said Dee, 'right here, it's them!'

She stopped, so quickly I almost ran through her as she came back down to my level. I could hear splashing, and someone talking quickly, urgently.

'Come on,' she said, and we pushed through the last line of bushes. We came out on a clearing filled with a wide, shining pool of water, its edges marked by some dark red fern. Light spilled down onto the water, which rippled and splashed as someone moved through it. Garth was sitting on a rock nearby, and he jumped up when he saw us, his face creased with worry.

'Dee, finally! I knew you'd come.'

'How long?' she said.

'Last night, and some times before then. I didn't say, but I should have, I know ...'

I looked out into the water. Danny was swimming, diving down into the pool, moving silently under the water, breaking the surface with a gleeful gasp, tumbling back down again.

'What the hell's he doing? Danny! Hey, Flipper!'

He turned, saw us, grinned and waved at me, and pushed off towards us.

'What's up with this?' I said. Garth shook his head.

'He wouldn't leave! He fought me when I tried to – when I said we should—'

'He fought you?'

'He said he *likes* it here.'

'Well, so do I, but you don't see me—'

A splash of water, cool but not icy, hit the side of my face. Danny's giggle filled the silent clearing, and he folded his arms up on the bank, still treading water, stirring up golden silt.

'Thanks for that,' I said, wiping my eyes.

'You guys should get in!' he said. 'It's incredible. This place is – I mean, wow.'

'Maybe you should get out,' I said. 'Aren't we going to get the book of spells?'

He kicked off again, swimming on his back, floating lazily away from us.

'Danny! You're – where's your clothes, man?'

I turned away, feeling myself blushing, my cheeks prickling with heat. I laughed.

'Dude, you're – you're not wearing anything!'

'So? Why should I? We can do what we want, Phil. Join me!'

'Hell, no.'

I heard another splash, the sound of water hitting grass, and Danny pulled himself out of the pool, shaking his head, wiping his face.

'Good as new!' he said.

'Danny, I told you, we shouldn't be here too long,' said Garth. He sounded worried, more worried than I'd thought,

187

and he wrung his hands together in front of him. 'It's not *good* to be here, to do this – I said, I told you—'

'I know what you said,' Danny muttered. 'I don't accept it. So there.'

'"So there"? You're not five, Danny. Listen to 'em!'

I kept my head down, my back to him. 'And put some bloody clothes on, you gimp.'

He'd moved nearer to me, I could feel it, could see him out of the corner of my eye. Drops of water hit the earth like rain.

'Or should I be taking pictures to show around school?'

He shrugged. 'Lucky school, eh? We could make a calendar. The Rugby Lads. We'd be rich.'

'Hit your head on the dive down, did you?'

'Oh, nice,' he said. 'I thought we were best friends? What's wrong with this?'

'You're an idiot,' I said.

'Phil—'

'Philippa! If we're such best friends, maybe you could learn my actual name?'

He smiled, not nicely, and a rush of anger made me look him in the eyes.

'Put your pants on and let's go, Tarzan.'

Garth and Dee were watching us nervously. Neither of them spoke.

'No,' said Danny.

'No?'

'No,' he said again.

He spread his arms wide and I looked away again, stifling a laugh.

'This!' Danny said. 'The World Between is ... is magic, isn't it? It's like nothing I've ever seen! You know that, how could you not want to stay? What more is there that we haven't even seen yet, haven't explored? What happens if you go west for a week? What happens if you go north? What's beyond the mountain, the forest, the stars? I will *know* this world, I will live in it, I will breathe it in and eat it and ... gah! How can you not just *want* it?'

'It isn't right.'

'They told you that, did they?' He flicked his head at the spectres. Dee met his gaze. Garth shook his head and stepped closer.

'I said, I told you, this place isn't meant for people, you'll burn up here, Danny! Flames are bad places for moths.'

'Moth, eh? Just a dumb little insect?'

'I didn't mean—'

'You can't make me leave. You can't! I get how this place works. Rules are different, right?'

'What rules?' I said. 'This isn't even real, Danny – we're in your room at home! You're on your bed!'

His eyes were wild, and he was moving, fidgeting, walking back and forth. 'My room. My dull, grey, boring room. Gee, what a ride.'

'You're an asshole.'

'Danny,' said Dee, 'you promised you'd help us. We need you. OK?'

He frowned in confusion. 'Promised?'

'Yes. We asked for help and you said you would. The book. Garth knows where it is but Philippa shouldn't go alone, should she?'

'I guess not.'

'It's dangerous, probably. Those people could hurt her.'

He looked at me and his expression softened. 'They can't,' he said.

'But they might,' I said. 'I'll go alone if I have to, but why don't you come back? Please?'

He looked down at himself, twisted to look back at the pool, its water calm and flat again. He looked at the trees, and the sky, and the rays of amber light that were flooding the world with colour. He smelled the air, and curled his toes into the earth.

'I don't want to,' he said.

'You can't always have what you want,' said Dee. Danny's frown flickered, and then he blinked, shook his head, rubbed his eyes.

'But this place – Phil, here it's just ... it's pure! Where's your mobile? Exams? TV? All those bloody stresses, those stupid problems, the teachers, school, Mum and Dad, getting a proper job, wearing a proper suit, all that ... all that rubbish. Where? Nowhere. There's just this place, and you, and me, and ... '

He had tears in his eyes, his voice cracking as he tried to speak, tried to make me see what he saw.

'I'm me here,' he said. 'Just me. Just me.'

'Please,' I said, holding his gaze. 'Please, Danny. This *isn't* you. I don't like it. Just come back. Come back, yeah?'

I reached out and touched his arm. 'Say you'll come and help?'

The air felt static, charged up with something, and then a gust of cool wind made me shiver. A pressure lifted, like the calm after a storm, and Danny blinked again.

'What ... what am I doing?' he said. 'What am I *doing*? Phil, don't look!'

He pushed me away, covering himself, crouching down.

'Yes! There he is!' said Garth. He looked at Dee. 'See you back there,' he said, and he put his hands on the sides of Danny's head, closed his eyes, and they were gone, nothing but empty space and wet footprints on the ground.

'Dee, what happened to him?'

'Too much sugar makes kids do crazy things,' she said.

'Very deep.'

'Thank you.'

'He'll be OK?'

She knelt down and touched the soil, smelled the red ferns that circled the pool. 'I don't know. I hope so. Think of this place as a drug and it might make things clearer. Don't you want to stay?'

'Well, yeah, but not forever.'

She smiled. 'Good. That's good. Remember that. Even a holiday in heaven would get tiring after a while.'

'Forgive me if I don't believe a spirit of Death about how dull heaven is.'

'True,' she said, solemn and serious. She stood up and took a deep breath.

'I think we've given them enough time.'

She moved closer, took my hand, and the World Between spun away, nothing but wind and shadows.

I was sitting on Danny's bed. Garth came in when he heard me cough, and waited for me to blink, get my balance, clear my head, before he spoke.

'Danny's in the shower. We should wait downstairs, I think.'

I jumped off the bed, ignoring the piles of clothes, the warmth where Danny had been sitting. I put my head in my hands and groaned. 'Oh, this is going to be awkward. How is he?'

'I think the phrase was *so embarrassed, I want to die, can't you just kill me if you're Death*?'

'Sounds about right. I'll make some coffee for him.'

Downstairs in the kitchen I searched through cupboards to find where things were. It felt weird opening drawers, pulling out cups, without Danny's parents around. My eyes kept darting out the window into the garden, worried that someone would see, that someone was watching. I found what I needed and the smell of coffee, bitter and oily, filled the house. I tried to calm down.

'We should have been more careful,' Dee said.

'Danny's not usually like this. I mean, he's a normal kid.'

She didn't reply, turned her head to watch the trees outside sway in a silent breeze.

'Why did Garth let him?'

She looked back. 'It's not that he let him. It's that Danny is strong. We're joined to you two, you know. Garth to Danny. Me to you. It goes both ways. I can take you to the World Between, but I can't force you there, or to leave. Danny ... worked that out.'

The coffee machine beeped once, twice, to let us know it was done. I heard footsteps on the stairs and turned to see Danny coming in, his hair still wet, his face flushed.

'Feeling better?' I said. He groaned, not looking me in the eye.

'Mate, forget it. It's fine. It's kind of funny, you know.'

'I don't want to talk about it.'

'OK. But I get how nice it is there, that place – I do.'

'You weren't the one running around without— Oh, man.' He put his face in his hands. 'Bloody hell.'

I poured his drink for him and set it down next to his head.

'There, there,' I said. 'It's not like I'm going to be selling pictures.'

'Phil!'

I slapped the back of his head.

'Ow! What the hell?'

'Philip*pa*, moron.'

'Fine, fine! Urgh.'

I found some bread and made toast. We ate it with butter and raspberry jam, and slices of apple cut up with a cheese knife.

'Feeling better?'

'I want to die.'

'You can do that later. We have a mission, remember? These two need to get to ... wherever it is they're going.'

'Home,' said Garth.

'Exactly.'

Danny made a groaning sound and kept his eyes closed.

'I didn't skip school to watch you mope just 'cause we all saw you ... strutting about.'

If anything, Danny turned redder, but at least he opened his eyes to scowl at me.

'I know where the book is,' said Garth. 'I can take you there.'

'We'll have to steal it back,' I said.

'Yes.'

'Like, break in and properly steal it. Like a crime.'

'Is that OK?' said Dee.

'I kind of feel like it has to be,' I said. 'Right? There's not another way, is there?'

Garth and Dee looked at each other, looked at me, watched Danny as he sat up again.

'How are we going to steal it?' he said.

'What do you mean?'

'Well, I can't pick locks. Can you?'

'No, but, we might not need to.'

'But what if we do?'

'I don't know! We have to try, right?'

'We can't put you in danger,' said Garth. 'If you don't want—'

'It's fine,' said Danny, waving Garth's words away. 'Whatever. It is. I just want us to know, all of us, how hard this is. We could get caught by the police. Or by them! What would they do?'

'We left their friend . . . just standing there,' I said, and I shivered, remembering the empty eyes, the blank, frightened face of the woman.

'Forget her,' said Danny. He stood up. 'It's a fight, isn't it? Them and their magic, trying to make people do what they want, and us, trying to stop them. We're the good guys.'

'OK.'

'But the good guys don't always win.'

'We will,' I said.

Danny took another bite of toast and rubbed his hands on his jeans. 'Right. Good. Come on then, Garth – where the hell's this book?'

Garth closed his eyes, his lips moving soundlessly. He

tapped his fingers, once, twice, three times, then nodded and smiled.

'A house, the other side of town. Whykam Road. They hid it in the library. I know the shelf.'

Danny's phone was already in his hand. 'Whykam Road,' he muttered, flicking through pages, typing in the address. He frowned when the answer came up. 'That's a three-hour walk. Wait – we can take a bus, it's like forty minutes.'

'A bus to a burglary?' I said.

'You want to walk?'

'Well, no.'

'Then we'll get the bus. It's fine.'

He jumped up, rubbing his hands through his hair. 'I need five minutes,' he said. 'Then we can head off.'

'Need help?'

'I'm good. Garth, coming with?'

Garth nodded, and the two of them headed back upstairs.

'They're not going to go . . . there?' I asked Dee.

'I don't think so. Not right now. Garth's not that gullible.'

'And Danny's not that stupid.'

She laughed, floating over the kitchen table to the other side of the room. 'You're sure about that?'

I put the butter and jam away and waited by the front door for Danny to come back.

ELEVEN

THE NUMBER eleven bus snaked its way across town, the windows rattling with the thrum of the engines. We sat at the back, staring, watching the buildings sail past. We were the only ones on the top deck – but it was the middle of a school day, so that wasn't much of a surprise.

'Good thing about being a spectre,' said Danny as we turned the corner past a park I'd ever seen before.

'Hmm? What's that?'

'Don't have to pay for your tickets.'

'If I could hold money,' said Garth, 'I would happily pay. I like buses. They're fun.'

'This is your first time!'

'And I'm having a ball.'

Danny snorted, not nastily, and went back to watching the streets. His phone beeped and he glanced at it.

'Five more stops,' he said. 'About fifteen minutes.'

My stomach tightened again. Dee and Garth scooted nearer. 'I'll point out the building,' said Garth. 'I see it all in her memories: how to get there, where the book is, how to get it. Piece of cake.'

'Right,' I said. 'Sure.'

'We can go ahead and check the coast is clear,' said Dee. 'And keep a look-out. Then once you've got it, we have to find somewhere to be alone, so we can ... well, so we can use it and get home.'

'Might be hard to find somewhere around here,' said Danny, 'just 'cause we don't know it. But if we bring the book back—'

'Can't use the house by the sea, though,' I said. 'They'd know to look there, right?'

'Right.'

'Four stops,' said Danny. The bus pulled to the side of the road, the door hissed, someone downstairs laughed, and we pulled away again. 'Thirteen minutes,' said Danny.

'We're getting ahead of ourselves,' said Garth. 'Don't worry about the ceremony. Just get the book, yeah?'

I fiddled with the zip on my jacket. My palms felt cold and sweaty.

'When you're gone,' I said, 'will that be it?'

I felt them all looking at me. The hum of the bus seemed to fade away. It was like I'd said something terrible, admitted something that we'd all agreed would be secret.

'We shouldn't be here,' said Dee. 'We shouldn't exist.

We're part of something bigger, cut off and forced to survive. It's not right. We have to go back.'

'And you can't follow,' said Garth. 'Not yet. Not yet, I hope.'

Danny's expression darkened. He waved his phone. 'Two more stops. We just went past that last one. We should get off and walk, probably. Philippa, ring the bell, will you?'

It felt like we were in another world. The streets, the shops, were as foreign to me as another country.

'How far away are we?' I said.

'Not that far. Weird, right?'

'How did I never know there was all of this right here?'

'The world's a lot bigger than we think,' said Danny, his voice getting lower.

'Thanks, Columbus.'

'Any time. Right, see that street up there? Next to the post office? That's Whykam. Garth, you got this?'

Garth sprang forward, bowing his head slightly as he focused on his thoughts on a world we couldn't see.

'Yes,' he said. 'This is it. We turn down there and it's on the left, big house, dark red brick, holly bushes both sides of the path. Number thirty-six.'

'You know all that?'

He tapped his head and grinned. 'Instant download.'

I didn't smile back. 'That woman—' I said.

'Wanted to hurt us,' said Danny. 'Come on, Philippa.'

'Oh, now he gets it right.'

Danny did a small bow. 'Always happy to serve.'

I rolled my eyes, but he knew I was pleased. We kept walking, up to the post office, around the corner and on to Whykam Road. Garth pointed ahead. 'There,' he said. 'We have to get there.'

I followed his finger and took a deep breath. The house was big – three floors at least, maybe even more – with different sized windows cut in to its walls, its roof, what looked like a tower. The bricks were a faded terracotta red, the woodwork painted black and shiny, the holly bushes clipped neatly into rows. I held back, already feeling exposed. I tugged on Danny's jacket.

'Want to hold hands?' he said.

'Shut up. Do you think they can see us? We need to wait.'

'A quick tumble in the bushes, then?'

'Danny, shut up. You're an idiot.' I called to Dee, and she ran back, calling Garth as she did.

'We shouldn't get too close, right?' I said. 'Not until you've checked who's in. Can you? See if anyone's watching from the windows.' I looked around, saw a small side road that cut between two buildings. 'We'll wait here,' I said. 'Search the rooms, make sure you know where everyone is.'

'Do you want to salute?' asked Danny. I punched him on the arm and pulled him towards the alley.

'We'll be back. Don't worry,' said Garth, and in a flash

he was gone. Dee nodded, her face serious and blank, and then she followed him, zipping towards the house, leaving us alone. I leaned against the wall and rubbed my eyes with my palms.

'You hit me,' said Danny.

'Sometimes you deserve it.'

'I was just joking around.'

'Don't worry, so was I.'

He opened his mouth to answer, stopped, frowned a little. He reached into his pocket and brought out his phone. I saw the screen flash. One new message.

'Anyone interesting?'

He didn't look up from reading the screen. 'Hmm? Oh. Um, it's Paul. Wanted to know where I am.'

'Oh. What'll you say?'

'Don't worry, not that I'm with you.'

'You can tell him whatever you want.'

It was back again, the tension, the strange static in the air that made things feel wrong and stalled. Danny and I had always been able to talk, to chat without thinking or worrying about things, but now everything was different. The easiness had melted away, and suddenly there were thorns on the path we'd been down so many times before.

'I tell them not to tease you,' he said, quieter than before, his fingers moving to respond to Paul's message.

'I don't care what they do. But thank you.'

'They're not losers, you know. They're good guys.

Scott's brother's a soldier, did you know? He went to Iraq. Asif can play the piano better than anyone. They're really cool.'

He sounded so young suddenly, so raw and nervous, that I didn't know what to say.

'Um. I didn't know that.'

'No, you didn't. You just see *rugger buggers* and think they're not worth anything.'

'Paul doesn't help himself, you know, the way he acts, what he says.'

Danny shrugged, his shoulders scratching against the brick wall. 'He's just a guy.'

'You know that's not fair,' I said.

The crackle of static, the tingle of a storm about to burst. Danny looked up at me and slipped his phone back into his pocket.

'You know what I meant.'

'Just one of the guys,' I said. 'Sure. I get it. How's Paul doing?'

'He's fine. I told him I'm sick.'

'Oh. Good.'

Minutes passed. Danny kicked at the dust on the floor. I could hear my heart beating in my chest, in my ears. I closed my eyes and tried to breathe in, and out, in, and out.

'That place,' said Danny, 'that World Between. Do you—'

He stopped, stood straight, nudged me in the side.

'What? Why—'

I opened my eyes and jumped. Dee was floating in front of me, her head cocked, a thin smile on her face.

'Sleeping on the job?'

'Kids these days,' said Garth, coming into the alley to stand next to her. I looked at Danny, but he was watching Garth, waiting to hear what they'd seen.

'Good news,' said Dee. 'Only two people in the house, both upstairs. The library's on the ground floor round the back – if they don't move, you've got a clean shot. The book's right there where Garth said. Oh, we're so close.' She was buzzing with energy, with excitement and nerves.

'Round the back?' said Danny.

'Through the front garden and down the side of the house,' said Garth. 'Then – through the window, I guess.'

'Break in, you mean.'

'I do.'

'No worries.'

'Oh, yeah, no worries,' I said. 'Breaking and entering, do this every day.'

'It's just glass, it'll smash.'

I rolled my eyes. 'You say that like it's an awesome answer.'

'Well then, what do you suggest?'

Dee's eyes were wide with hope. Garth's dark skin shone in the light. I shook my head.

'It's what we have to do,' I said. 'I get that. Fine. Just . . . don't be so casual.'

'Hey,' said Danny, grinning and giving me a thumbs-up, 'I'm bad to the bone, me.'

'My hero. Ready?'

He jumped from one foot to the other. 'OK. Yes. Let's do this.'

'We'll be your eyes,' said Dee. 'Just keep going straight. You won't be seen.'

Danny put his hand on my shoulder. 'We can do this.'

'If we get caught, I'm turning you in, police deal style.'

He nodded. 'I would expect nothing less. I'd do well in prison.'

'Pretty boy like you, I'm sure.'

He winked. 'You think I'm pretty?'

I moved my arm, pushing his hand off. 'Enough of that. On three, OK?'

'OK.'

'Roger, roger,' said Garth. Dee nodded and rose higher off the ground.

'One,' I said. I could hear a bird chirping nearby. 'Two.' A motorbike revved and faded away. 'Three.' A breeze blew, the wind cold on my cheeks. 'Go!' I hissed, and we ran out from the alley, crossing the road at a run and moving towards the house.

'Faster!' said Danny, keeping his voice low. 'Don't slow down!'

We were level with the holly bushes. I paused at the end of the path that led to the front door, but Dee was ahead of me, calling me forward.

'You're clear, come on!'

'Come on!' Danny said, pushing past me and moving to the right. I followed him, the gravel beneath our feet crunching like old bones. Along the side of the house there was a thin corridor of space, and we moved down it, jumping over piles of bricks, forgotten bags of leaves.

'No one can see you,' said Garth.

'Hang on,' said Danny, and we stopped, ducking down in the shade between a wooden fence and the cold brick of the side of the house. Ahead was a wooden gate, taller than both of us, but thin and wobbly.

'Locked?' said Danny.

'We can get over that,' I said.

'I know I can.'

'And so can I! Come on.'

We sprang forward again, and I watched as Danny tested his weight on the grey wood. It rocked a little when he pulled himself up, but the door was shut from the other side. He swung his leg over and for a second he stopped, perched on top like a mounted rider, looking down into the garden. Then, without looking back, he was gone, sliding down and landing with a soft thud on the other side.

'Now you,' he said.

'Gee, you think so?'

I heard him laugh from behind the door. The wood was rough and covered in a thin, dusty moss, but I pulled myself up and got my knee over. Danny was standing staring into the garden, and as I landed next to him he crouched down, biting his lip, putting his hands on the thin grass.

'Is anyone looking this way?' he asked. Garth floated forward and up around the corner of the house. We watched him as he backed away, staring at the windows overlooking the grass.

'No,' he said. 'One guy's at a desk, reading. There's a woman on a computer, but her back's to the window.'

'Clear shot,' muttered Danny.

'Dee, which window leads to the library?'

We shuffled forward, keeping low, wincing at every sound. Halfway across the face of the house Dee stopped and pointed. 'There. See that bookshelf? Halfway up, there's a box that's disguised as a dictionary. Open it up and the book's in there.'

We peered in. The room was mostly dark, the door closed, varnished wooden tables and shelves sucking in any light that made it through the glass. Rows of books, their covers cracked and worn, lined three sides. Papers and pencils were scattered on the main table. It looked like someone had been studying and lost their temper. I focused on the window. The glass looked old and thin, the frame built of wood and metal rather than plastic.

'Looks weak enough,' said Danny.

'Well, it's glass.'

'So – you want to do it?'

He looked around, saw something on the ground, picked it

up and raised his eyebrows. In his hand, round and smooth and dull, was a rock.

'Um, you go ahead.'

A flash of doubt crossed his face. I could see the sheen of sweat on his forehead.

'Yeah,' he said. 'Right. Yeah.'

His eyes flicked from Dee to Garth, and a new hardness, something resolute, set his features.

'We've got to help you guys,' he said. It wasn't a question. Garth nodded. Dee watched them both. A strange smile crept onto Danny's face.

'For Frodo!' he said, and he raised the rock above his head.

The glass smashed into dagger-thin shards, scattering onto the floor like ice. I jumped, gasping at the sound, but Danny moved quickly, reaching through the broken pane and flipping up the window latch. He pulled his arm out and began sliding the window up, and together we pushed until there was enough room to get through.

'Grab the book!' said Danny, perching on the ledge to take the full weight. 'I'll hold this open. Go!'

I stuttered something, my heart racing as I clambered into the room. Glass crunched beneath my feet and I slid a little, catching myself by grabbing the nearest table.

'They heard,' said Dee. 'They're coming. Quickly!'

I swore and ran across the room. Danny said something, but I couldn't hear him, couldn't make sense of what he meant. Dee was right beside me.

'Here,' she said, urgent and quiet, 'over here. Third shelf up. See the blue book? The dictionary?'

I reached out and pulled the book down. It was heavy – heavier than it should have been. I opened the cover, revealing the hollow insides of a wooden box. A thick, dark green book was resting on soft material padding.

'Grab it!' said Dee. 'That's it! Come on!'

'Hurry up!' said Danny. I heard him grunt as he shifted his position. Someone was shouting upstairs, and then footsteps thudded on wooden steps. I grabbed the book, dropping the box with a clatter, and turned back towards the window. Danny's eyes were fixed on me, and he was swearing under his breath.

'Phil, for God's sake, come on!' he spat.

More shouting, and someone running. I ran to the window, climbing out past Danny, and I smelled sweat and grass and earth. There was a drop of blood soaking into the wooden frame, and a trickle running from Danny's palm, down along his wrist.

'You're hurt!'

He let go of the window, jumping down into the garden. The frame slammed down, shattering another pane, the sound impossibly loud.

'It's nothing! Come on!'

'Stop!' shouted a man. 'Stop them!'

'Run!' shouted Danny, and without another word we bolted for the garden door. Danny was first, climbing desperately, leaving a smear of blood on the wood. I waited for him to jump down before pulling myself up, the book clutched in one hand, my hair stuck to my face, getting in my eyes.

'Here,' I said, throwing the book down. 'Keep going.'

He picked the book up and took a few steps, then stopped, waiting for me. I grunted and climbed down, landing awkwardly, steadying myself with my hands. Together we raced down the alley, onto the driveway and towards the road away from the house.

We skidded to a halt. At the end of the path, blocking our way out, a group of men and women were staring at us mid-stride, their faces frozen in surprise. There were ten of them maybe, all old, all dressed in expensive clothes. Nobody spoke. I felt like the world had shuddered to a stop – that nothing would ever move again. I couldn't understand what was happening, what this meant. Something shattered in the house behind us, and like a bullet through glass, the sound broke our stand-off. Danny swore, and the men and women moved forward, their faces twisting into smiles, frowns, looks of confusion.

'Back, back!' shouted Danny.

'They're coming out the house,' said Garth, and I spun round to see the front door opening, a man stepping out, his face red with rage.

'Stop them!' he screamed, pointing his finger at us. 'They have the book! They have the book!'

The scrape and crunch of footsteps on gravel, and the group was running for us, spreading out to block the way.

'Garth, get them!' said Danny. 'Get their heads!'

'But – all of them? I can't—'

I screamed as someone clamped down a hand on my shoulder. A woman had come out from the house, silent, her eyes wide with anger and glee, and she pulled me hard towards her.

'Ow! Get off!'

Someone was shouting – Dee, close by, and Garth, further away – and Danny was struggling against two large men, and a third was shouting at them, 'Take them inside! Quick, someone will see!'

'Who should I stop? Who?' shouted Garth. He was staying near to Danny, flittering back and forth. I could see the road, the stretch of pavement through the holly bushes, and I screamed for help, screamed as loud as I could. An icy hand, thin and strong, clamped down on my mouth, the force knocking my teeth together, and I tasted blood on my lips. It was an impulsive, angry slap. My scream caught in my throat. I struggled, desperate to breathe, and I was pulled faster, my feet scrabbling and slipping on the gravel, and then we were inside the house, and the light was filled with shadows, and the sound of a door shutting echoed with grim finality. Where was Danny? The woman let go of my mouth and I twisted my head to see. He was in front, pulled by three of the group, shouting and spitting at them. One of the men – his hair was thin and lay flat on his head – raised a hand and thumped him around the ear.

'Quiet, you idiot!'

'No!' I shouted.

The man looked back. 'Oh, hurry up and get them into the blue room. I can't stand this.'

A door on our right was kicked upon – it was the room before the library, I guessed, which meant it looked out on the side of the house – and we were bundled in, sweating and shaking, while one by one the men and women followed. The door was locked, the key slipped into a pocket, and then, as if by command, the room fell deathly silent.

TWELVE

'Y<small>OU</small>,' <small>SAID</small> one of the women, 'are the children who disturbed us the other day, when we had hoped to carry out the ritual.'

'Don't know anything about a ritual,' said Danny. 'Don't say anything,' he added, looking at me.

'You do know,' said the woman, 'because you came back for this.' She held up her hand, flourishing the book.

'Don't know what you're on about,' said Danny. 'We called the police. You're screwed.'

One of the men looked nervous. He shuffled his feet and cleared his throat. 'Um, Susan, isn't this a bit ...? I mean, they're children, and this is ... well it *is* kidnapping, so to speak. I'm not sure—'

'Quiet, George. No backing down now. We have a deal to make.'

'Yes, but—'

'Oh, do be quiet!' hissed someone else. I looked at Danny,

trying to think what to say, what to do. Dee was beside me, her eyes shining, her fists clenched.

'If they hurt you . . . ' she said, and she shook her head. 'I'm ready.'

I looked around the room. The men and women were shuffling and nervous, their anger falling away now we were in the house. A few of them glanced at the woman by the door. I remembered her. I remembered what she wanted.

'Where did you get it?' I asked.

'Phil!' hissed Danny. The woman smiled coldly and clicked her nails together.

'Hmm. Somewhere far away. It took me a long time.'

'I know what it is. I know you killed for it. I know what you think you're doing.'

'Oh? And how do you know that?'

I tried to smile casually, and settled for a brief smirk. She watched me without blinking.

'Why did you come to the school?' I said.

'To find you, of course. As you said, you know *so* much. We can't let things fall apart now, when we're so close, when we were so ready.'

'You're wrong,' said Danny. Blood was dripping from the cut on his hand. 'You don't know what you're doing. You're mental. It's dangerous.'

When she spoke, Susan's voice was high, hysterical, laughter bubbling from somewhere deep inside her.

'And what do you know of what we're doing?'

'Why don't you tell us?' I said.

'Adult things.'

'That just means stupid things.'

'You think so?' she laughed. 'Then what are you up to? Why do you want this?'

She shook the book like a rattle, and the adults standing around us murmured uneasily.

Dee looked nervous. 'Don't let them know,' she hissed.

'Just wanted to know what it is,' I said.

'You just wanted to know?'

'Yeah.'

Susan sighed and finally looked away. In a whisper, too quiet to hear, she spoke to a woman on her left, who nodded and moved towards the door. She pulled the key from her pocket, opened the door, left the room and locked it again.

'Now even if we take care of them all you'll still be trapped in here,' said Garth.

'Not if we break the window,' said Danny. The woman frowned.

'I'm sorry?'

Danny winced at his mistake. 'Death,' he said. 'You want to control Death. That's what you said, right?'

That same smile, distant and fake, a thin line of white teeth between her pale lips.

Danny frowned, and I knew he was trying to understand. 'Why?'

One of the men laughed, spluttering slightly. 'Why? You really are just a kid. You've never known pain, not really. You've never felt loss. That's the word, you know – loss. When someone is ripped from you, and you're just ... a walking wound, a void. Death. Taking and taking from us, and why? Because he can?'

'She,' I said. The man's eyes moved over me as if I wasn't there.

'We will control Death and we will have our answers. We will have our *justice*.'

'A safer world,' said someone else, nodding, 'that's it. End to all this violence. End to all this madness. Safety. Happiness. Think about it! Think about that!'

'We're not bad people,' said a woman standing near to me. I looked at her, at her uncombed hair, the way she fiddled with the ring on her finger, the way she looked at me, kindly, almost scared. 'We want to *fix* things. But this – this wasn't really what we wanted, this mess.' She spoke up. 'Susan, don't you think this is ... too much?'

Danny was getting restless beside me. Garth was saying something to him, and he nodded and stretched his fingers, curled them into a ball.

By the door, Susan lowered her head, her posture shifting, and she wiped her eyes with her fingers. She looked so tired suddenly, so different, that I thought she might faint.

'It wasn't supposed to be this way, no,' she said. 'So ... complicated. The world is cruel and callous and uncaring.

I want you to know that, children. I want you to know what real life is.'

This felt wrong, the way she spoke, the looks from the others. A knot of fear, like cold electricity, sparked in my stomach. 'Dee,' I muttered, 'Dee, please . . . '

'But,' said one of the men, 'if you can help, then even now, we will . . . back down.'

'Help you?' spat Danny. 'Help you do this? Kill people and . . . and stop Death?'

The man shook his head. Susan raised her hands. 'Please,' she said, 'please.'

'She looks so tired,' said Dee. Susan took a step forward, bending so that we were face to face. Danny tensed. Dee moved closer. Susan's breath smelled of mint and something else, something bitter.

'It's not us you need to help. I want you to help *her*.'

'Her who?'

Without looking, she reached behind and rapped her knuckles on the door. The lock clicked, the handle turned, and the woman with the key stepped in, bringing someone with her, leading them by the hand. As she stepped through the door I gasped, taking a small step back, and Danny let out a long, low sigh. The room was tense now, everyone watching us, their postures changing, hostile, scared, stepping back, moving forward. Dee stepped sideways to stand next to Garth.

'Oh, no,' she said. Garth's face was blank.

Standing in front of us, a distant smile on her face, her head turned towards the ceiling, was the woman from yesterday. They led her slowly, like a nervous animal. She smiled at them vaguely.

'Barbara. Barbara. Here, pet. Over here.'

Susan's voice was soft and gentle, the voice you use to talk to a child. My stomach felt tight, my head achy. What had we done to her? She stared at the ceiling, let herself be led slowly into the room.

'There's no point,' said someone. 'We need to take her to a hospital, for God's sake!'

'This isn't normal, though,' said a thin man – Cully, I thought – with his hands clasped behind his back. Susan stepped towards us, past the dazed woman. She patted her arm gently and smiled at her.

'We're not monsters,' she said, focusing on Danny. I smelled something else on her – perfume, vanilla and something else, something sweet. I liked it. Susan cleared her throat.

'We don't know what this is. What did you do? What is this – some other magic?'

I opened my mouth but Danny nudged me. 'I'm sorry about her. She was trying to catch us.'

Susan knelt down a little, hands on her legs.

'I have an important question. One that I want you to answer honestly. Can you make her better?'

Danny flicked his eyes to Garth, who'd moved closer to

the woman, almost touching her. He moved his hands slowly in front of her face, her vacant eyes, her frozen smile.

'I think so,' he said. He looked at Dee, called her over. They whispered to each other, shot looks at us, moved around the woman, weighing her up.

'Well?' said Susan, still staring down at Danny. Then, swallowing as if it tasted bad in her mouth, she added, 'Please?'

'She doesn't deserve this,' said Cully. He raised his voice, spoke to the whole room. 'When we all signed up, this was never . . . I mean, injury, maybe, or death, but not this . . . this purgatory.'

'I'm so sorry,' I said. 'We didn't mean to – it wasn't a plan, we just—'

'We can help her,' said Danny, 'but—'

Susan held up her hand, and our eyes followed the book. 'We'll give you this. Don't look so shocked. It doesn't matter now. We'll give you the book – it's what you came for, right? – if you'll help her, if you'll make her better. That's it. The book for her mind.'

Dee moved back to stand between me and Danny. 'You really think she means it?'

I shrugged, moving as little as I could.

'I don't trust them,' said Garth, 'but if they let you guys go, it's worth a shot. I . . . I think I can do it. Undo it, I mean. I don't know. I have to. I will. And we need the book, Dee. We need it.'

'But what if we just help her and they keep the book anyway?'

'We can't trust you,' I said. The group muttered and scowled. Susan nodded and stood up straight, folding her hands.

'Can we trust you? Look what you did! You're hiding something, aren't you? You have power. Don't pretend, girl.'

We were both breathing hard. Garth frowned and turned to Dee. 'I can do this,' he said. 'I know I can control it. If I . . . if I concentrate. Yes.'

'And then there's one extra person to keep them trapped,' she said. 'I don't like it.'

Susan tapped her foot against the wooden floor. 'Well?' she said. 'A fair trade. That's what we ask.'

'Tell them you'll do it in the driveway,' said Garth. 'They give you the book, I undo what I did, and we're off. They can chase us if they like – you think these old guys are faster than us?'

Danny looked at me, raised his eyebrows. *Well?*

I looked around the room, at the faces of the strangers. They were tired, confused, scared. In the centre of the room, Barbara was humming softly, her arms swinging back and forth. She stared at nothing. I nodded.

'We'll stay together,' said Dee, moving even nearer to me. 'If we have to fight again, I'll be ready.'

Danny was talking, giving our terms, telling them what to do. Susan hugged the book closer to her chest.

'If that's what you'd prefer,' she said, 'we can do so. We just want our friend back. This was never meant to happen.'

'Just a bunch of frightened fools,' said Dee, looking around the room. 'I don't buy it. This is a trick. Her words are thin and slippery.'

'Come,' said Susan, 'you want to do it in the driveway? We can do that. Come on. I'll lead.'

One by one, we walked slowly out of the room, squinting a bit as we walked back on to the gravel outside. Dee hovered close to me. I wondered if anyone would hear me if I screamed.

'If this is a trap . . . ' said Danny, and the woman nearest him looked shocked.

'Why would we risk it? Look at her! Enough. Enough of this.'

'But they want Death! They want to stop us,' said Dee.

'She means a lot to them,' said Garth. 'I have her memories, remember? They're really good friends. For years, I think.'

'You really think they'll give us the book?'

'I think so.'

Dee looked torn. 'Then we can go home,' she said. 'and this – all this, it will end.'

'Let's not get ahead of ourselves,' I said. We'd formed a semicircle now, Danny and I still hemmed in against the house. I nudged him and he leaned close.

'How do we do this?'

'They have to think it's us who have power,' he said. 'Make them afraid, yeah?'

'I don't know . . . '

'I'll do it,' he said.

'You sure?'

He stepped forward, raising his arms. 'I'm ready. Give the book here. Phil, take it.'

Susan and I walked towards each other. Wind whipped leaves around my feet. I met her eyes – still sharp and clear and suspicious – and put my hands out, waiting for her to hand it over. Behind her, someone muttered something. She hesitated, and my heart began to race, but then she smiled with fake sweetness and rested the book in my hands.

'It took me a long, long time to find that,' she said. 'I wouldn't let it go without good reason. You treat it well.'

I blinked, stepped away, and started moving back to Danny.

'No,' he said, and I stopped. 'No, you head out to the road. Make sure they're not . . . tempted, yeah?'

More muttering, men shaking their heads, but they parted for me to move through. Their eyes followed the book. It felt heavy in my hands, almost impossible to carry. I stood straight and moved towards the road.

'A deal's a deal,' said Susan. 'Please. Please. Help her. Help Barbara.'

Danny nodded and Garth sprang up. 'Happy to,' said Garth, and without another sound he plunged his fingers into the sides of her head. Her whole body tensed, her eyes rolling back, her fingers twitching. There were gasps, shouts, and the group rushed towards her. Garth stuck his tongue out, concentrating. Dee watched him, studying his movements, seeing something I could not. The group crowded around her, their faces frozen in horror and worry.

'What are you doing to her? You're killing her!'

'No . . . I'm . . . not!' said Garth. Danny was edging closer to me.

'I'm returning her memories,' he said. 'I'm doing what I promised.'

'Quite the little liar,' said Dee, her gaze never leaving Garth. Then, with a flourish, Garth let go, springing back as the woman crumpled to the ground. More shouts, someone swearing, and one of the men moved towards us.

'Bastards!' he said. 'You killed her! Little bastards!'

Danny's face was white, and now his voice shook a little. 'What? No! We – I mean, I – she should be—'

He backed away, raising his arms, shifting his feet to steady himself. Was he going to fight this guy?

'Danny!' I shouted.

In the middle of the clamouring group, someone gave a gasp, and a slight, shuddering moan. Barbara opened her eyes.

'What?' she said. 'Where – where am I? David? Why are you—'

As one, the group exploded in shouts, talking over each

other, trying to help her to her feet, give her room, explain what they had done. The man span around away from us, his face splitting into a grin, a strange sob catching in his throat.

'Oh, Barbara!' he shouted. He ran towards her.

'Time for us to go,' said Danny, grabbing my hand and starting to run. The last thing I saw before we burst onto the road was the cold, shining eyes of Susan, staring after us as she stood above Barbara, her hands clasped together, her lips curled in disgust.

We ran until our legs were shaking, until our lungs burned as if the air were acid. We took random turns, left, right, straight, through parks, between shops, until finally I had to stop, doubled over, panting and my head throbbing, resting my weight against a tree. Danny fell down next to me, his face shining.

'What,' I managed, 'the hell.'

'Just steal the book!' he said, and he laughed, a mad, near-hysterical burst of sound.

'But we did it!'

'Did it!' he repeated. I held the book up, then put it down next to me, too tired to even lift my arms.

'We have to keep moving,' he said. 'We have to get home, get this safe.'

'Well ...' I paused, breathing deeply, holding my side, 'where are we?'

He pulled out his phone, moving his fingers sluggishly, squinting in the light.

'There's a bus we can take from the end of this road,' he said. 'It'll get us near home. Come on.'

'Can't we rest? Just a minute more.'

He was already standing up, looking around, nervous and twitchy. 'I don't know ...'

'Oh, fine,' I said, and I pulled myself up. I reached for the book, and laughed when I saw Dee and Garth both kneeling over it, their heads low, almost touching the faded leather cover.

'Praying?'

They looked up, faces serious, eyes focused. 'Just trying to see what the fuss is,' said Dee, standing up and dusting something invisible off her shoulders.

'I mean, this book,' said Garth, 'it's ... unique. Magic. It shouldn't even exist. But it does, and we can go home because of it.'

'I thought you wouldn't even be here if it wasn't for it?' said Danny.

'Maybe,' said Garth.

'It and those people,' said Dee.

We stood awkwardly, not saying anything, not wanting to look at each other. It was still too raw – the fight, the blue room, the way they looked at Barbara. I cleared my throat. 'Which bus?' I said.

He checked his phone. 'Number 107. Should be a couple of minutes.'

'All right. We should head home. Then we can see what we need to do to ... y'know.'

'Get rid of the pests,' said Danny. Garth pulled a face.

'Oi!'

'I mean, banish the demons back to whence they came.'

'Demons are different,' said Dee coolly.

Danny stopped smiling.

'The bus,' I said again. 'Come on.'

We started walking again. I heard birdsong nearby, smelled cinnamon and butter drifting out from a bakery.

'My house'll be empty till this evening,' said Danny.

'Mine too.'

'Cool.'

A cloud passed in front of the sun, sending a chill across the town, a grey shadow that spread out, roads at a time.

'Are we going to need anything?'

'Hmm?'

Danny looked back over his shoulder at Garth. 'In the empty house, when we heard them first calling you, they had ... I don't know, offerings. Things to make it work. Will we need them?'

'You have us,' said Dee. 'That should be enough.'

'Oh.'

I flicked through the book. I couldn't understand a word.

'We'll help you,' said Garth. 'It'll be OK. You'll see. We'll be out of your hair before you know it!'

'That's good, at least,' I said. Danny didn't say anything.

Behind us I heard the low rumble of the bus engine. The stop was just ahead of us.

'Come on,' I said, 'hurry.'

We jogged, too lazy to run anymore. A few minutes later we were sitting on the backseat, hot and sweaty but free and safe, as the bus rumbled us home, and away from the house of the Society.

We sat at in Danny's kitchen, steaming cups of tea in front of us, a plate of biscuits surrounded by crumbs. Danny's hand was wrapped in a white bandage, a smear of dirt on his cheek. Garth stood behind him, Dee sat next to me. I opened the book and turned the pages slowly, letting her read the words, stopping when she asked, sometimes going back a few lines so she could double-check some point. She mumbled to herself, asked Garth questions, using words I couldn't understand, a language that didn't sound real.

'So what is this?' Danny said.

'Most of it's just theory,' said Garth. 'It's patchy at best, but it was written by him, the one who spoke to Death. Looks like he experimented. He managed to put together a viable summoning, a way of capturing a spirit – *the* spirit, Death, us, whatever – in a bind. Well, that's what it says. But you know what? I don't think it would work.'

'But it did!' said Danny, folding his arms.

'Did it? They managed to open a door, and we started coming through – but there's no record that anyone's ever got further than that, that they've actually made Death their servant. Think about it – if someone had, wouldn't you know? An unstoppable ruler doesn't just disappear from history.'

'So it doesn't even work,' I said.

'Even opening the door is . . . it's amazing he got this far. No wonder this book is worth fighting for. Even some of these things shouldn't be possible. Keep going, Philippa.'

I turned the next page, and Dee clapped her hands together. 'There!' she said. 'That's it – that's what we need!'

Garth leaned over, scanning the page, his face twisting into a manic grin. 'Oh, clever!' he said.

'What? What?' I said. The words made no sense to me – it was an impossible squiggle, curving and fluid, more like spilled and splattered ink than writing.

'It's the incantation to bridge the worlds!' said Garth.

'Which means it's our way home,' said Dee. 'Oh, Garth – we did it! We did it!'

They jumped up, dancing and twirling in the air, letting out whoops and shouts. Danny laughed as he watched them move around the room.

'So – we can do this?' I said. Dee kept on dancing.

'Soon!' she said. She looked back at the page. 'It needs moonlight and wood, and somewhere near water. And . . .

yes, enough space to draw a chalk circle. We can find some-where before tonight, right? Right?'

'Uh, sure,' I said. My mind was racing. Water? Wood? 'How big?' I said.

Dee looked around. 'Size of this room would work fine.'

'House by the cliff?' said Danny.

'Yeah, right. The Society knows about it, they're probably already looking for us.'

He scratched his chin. I noticed his thin moustache again, opened my mouth to say something, closed it and looked away. 'Something made of wood by a river, maybe? Or—'

'The pier,' he said.

'You think?'

'There's the old café halfway along. Wood floors. Empty. Safe.'

'Safe?'

'Well, mostly.'

'They closed it for a reason.'

'Isn't that, like, an insurance thing? It's been there for years. It's not going to fall down now.'

I thought of the pier, its damp, rotting wood jutting out into the sea, the seaweed staining its poles, the salt and the wind biting into its core.

'Maybe,' I said. 'Think you can get on, though?'

He shrugged. 'I've done it before.'

I blinked. 'What?'

'I mean, with some mates. We went there for dares. You

can get into the old buildings. They're mostly empty, just a load of rubbish and seagulls.'

'When did you go? What mates?'

He sighed. 'Philippa, come on. Just with Paul and everyone. It's no big deal.'

'No, I know. Just asking. It's just funny, you weren't so keen to explore the old house, were you?'

He looked at me, a thin smile on his lips, but then he nodded up at Garth and Dee, chattering away above our heads. 'And that worked out so well, eh?'

'Oh, come on,' I said. 'There was no way I could have known—'

'It's fine,' he said. He raised his voice. 'Garth, we could really do this tonight?'

'We could,' said Garth. 'This book's amazing. It lays it out. It's not even that difficult if you know the words, so long as you have the right place.'

'And you'd be ... gone? Gone back home, through this door?'

Garth and Dee floated back down, stopping when they were level with us.

'Yes. It's the right thing to do.'

'I know,' said Danny. 'Sure. Cool. What else do we need?'

Garth looked at Dee. She shook her head. 'Nothing. We can do this.'

Danny cleared his throat. He took a sip of tea, wiping his mouth with the back of his hand.

'It's been a mental few days,' he said. I watched the steam drift up from our cups, mingle through the air, flicker and disappear into the sunlight. A thin buzzing filled the air – Danny's phone shivered on the wooden table and he snatched it without looking.

'Paul,' he said, before I'd even asked. He looked surprised. 'He's outside?'

'What?'

He stood up, pushing his chair back with a screech. 'Said he was worried about me. He's nicked off at lunch and cycled here.'

'Oh, not now!'

'It's pretty nice of him.'

I tried to think of something to say, but Danny was already moving down the hall towards the front door.

'Wait, you're not going to answer it?'

He paused, looking back at me. 'Of course I am. Look, I know you don't like him—'

'So what? We've got other things to do right now!'

'I'll just be a min,' he said, smiling and shaking his head. He kept walking, reaching for the door.

'What? How can you—'

He opened the door, letting light and cold air pile into the hallway. For a second I stood there frozen, blinking in the brightness, and then I ducked back into the kitchen, resting my palms on the table, breathing deeply. Dee looked worried.

'He'll be back in a tick,' she said. 'I'm sure. He'll get rid of his friend.'

'We have stuff to do,' I said.

'We have until this evening.'

'But – we need to prepare! And we're meant to be here in secret, right? So why does Paul get to know what we're doing?'

'Danny won't tell him,' said Garth. He looked towards the front of the house. 'I'll go check. It'll be fine.'

We could hear voices from the hall now, Paul's laughter, Danny's reply. They were standing at the doorway.

'Danny should tell him he's sick,' I said. 'Make sure he does. And tell him he's an idiot.'

Garth saluted, jumping up and shooting out after Danny. I took another sip of my tea, and stole another biscuit. I pulled out my phone, checked that nothing fun was going on. Another burst of laughter in the hall, and then Danny coughing, obviously faking it. Paul said something else. Dee was watching me.

'What?' I asked, spitting crumbs onto the table.

'Nothing. Really.'

'He just doesn't see that they're using him,' I said. 'Danny's not some dumb, macho man.'

'And Paul is?'

'Ha! He wishes.'

'Oh.'

I flicked my thumb across the phone screen. Pictures of school friends, drama, gossip. I shut it off and put it back in my pocket. I heard the front door shut, and then feet on the stairs, moving quickly, almost stomping.

'Did he invite him in? What's he playing at?'

Dee closed her eyed, opened them. 'No, that other boy's gone. Danny's by himself.'

'Oh, good. Good. We have to get chalk, you said? And get to the pier and make sure it's safe. And you have to talk us through how this' – I nudged the book with my fist – 'is actually going to work.'

'And then,' Dee's face lit up, almost dreamy, 'home. Oh, home. Being here in the world is so ... I mean, it's not the same. Flat. It's too flat.'

'It works for me.'

She laughed. 'For now.'

I leaned forward, folding my arms on the table top. 'And then what? Can you tell me? Do you know?'

Her eyes were closed again, but the corners of her mouth turned up, like she remembered something from long ago.

'No spoilers,' she said. 'There's no way I could put it into words.'

'But you have to know something?'

She opened her eyes. 'I know a lot of things. Not all of them are for you, Philippa.'

I took another biscuit. 'Fine. Whatever. What even happens to you if we – I mean, when you ... go back?'

For the first time a flicker or something, sadness or fear, made Dee look away. 'We go back,' she said.

'Yeah?'

'And ... join up.'

I took a bite. 'Join ... Death?'

'We are Death, but just small parts, cut off, lost. We'll return, and be ... absorbed, I suppose.' She lowered her head slightly and stared at me, all traces of laughter gone from her eyes. 'There's only one Death, Philippa. Only one. Eternal and everywhere, joining and binding and touching all life. There's no sense of self, no different views and ways of doing things. We're part of that, and we'll go back to that.'

'But ... that's just dying, isn't it?'

She blinked, slowly, and looked at her hands. 'Death can't die,' she said.

'But – what about you and Garth? Your names, your lives? You'll just ... go away?'

'We've only lived for three days. It's not much.'

'It's enough,' I said. 'It's not right, what you're saying!'

'Believe me, it's perfectly right.'

'Well then, it's not fair.'

She didn't answer that. Danny's tea was going cold. I touched the mug with the back of my hand, glancing at the ceiling.

'If he's still in the bathroom we should start getting worried soon.'

'Maybe you should lay off the— Wait!'

Dee cocked her head, squinting as if she could hear something, sense something far off.

'What is it? Is it them?'

I jumped up, ran to the window to look out from behind the lace curtains. 'There's no one I can see,' I said. 'Danny! Hey, Danny!'

Dee was standing up, moving slowly into the hallway, her face hardening into a frown. 'He won't hear you,' she said.

'Oh, God. What? Why?'

She flicked her head upwards and pointed to the ceiling. 'He's gone,' she said.

'What do you mean, he's gone? Where's Garth?'

'He's gone, too,' she said. She called me towards her, a strange impatience making her twitch her fingers. 'They're up there, but they're gone. Oh, we shouldn't have left them alone. They've gone back to the World Between.'

Danny was lying on his bed, his head on his pillow, his eyes staring up at nothing. A smile was frozen on his face, a slice of white teeth showing. I shivered and looked down at him.

'Idiot,' I said.

'He waited till he could get away from us,' said Dee.

'Couldn't Garth just . . . not help him?'

A pause. 'I think he's managed to force Garth into it. I don't know.' She moved closer. 'Not good.'

'We have to go get him again, right?'

I looked at the clock on his bedside table. I flicked the curtains open and looked out on the street.

'Paul's gone. Had to get back to school.'

'We should do this now,' said Dee. 'They haven't been gone that long.'

I swore under my breath and sat down on the bed, taking Danny's hand. It was already cold.

'If you're naked again, I swear to God,' I said, looking at him. I felt cold panic in my stomach, and nodded at Dee.

'Come on,' I said, 'back through the looking glass.'

She gave me a funny look, reached out, and we fell through nothing and everything.

THIRTEEN

T HE AIR smelled of mint and sand. I stumbled, the ground moving beneath my feet, and put one hand down to steady myself.

'Careful,' said Dee. She kicked at the dirt. 'Sand. Look.'

To our left, stretching away until it fell into the horizon, dessert sand ebbed and flowed, golden in the light, purple in the shadows. It moved under our feet, shifting and hissing. Twilight was falling – I saw traces of stars in the sky, and the air held coolness mixed with the heat of the sand. Just where we stood, the sand stopped. Brown, cracked earth shone through, and then a few feet away the great forest leaned over us, the outer trees swaying and moaning, their needles falling and mixing with the dessert.

'We're at the edge here,' said Dee. 'That sand goes on forever, looks like.'

I closed my eyes. I felt the pull of the desert, the waves of heat, the pulse of the dunes. Things grew beneath me. I curled my toes in my shoe, felt a rush of joy. I opened my eyes.

'This place,' I said. 'It's alive. It's like lightning in your veins.'

'Lightning burns,' said Dee. She sighed. 'Lightning kills.'

I cupped my hands around my mouth. 'Danny! Danny!'

'The trees,' said Dee. 'Has to be. We'd see them if they'd gone into the dunes.'

'Why would he do this?'

'Same reason as before.'

'Can you find them?'

She shut her eyes, her breathing slowing slightly. 'Yes,' she said. She pointed into the darkness of the trees. 'That way. Moving quickly.'

We ran, ducking under the lowest branches, pushing our way through strings of vines and flowers. Above us, the clouds parted, and I saw swirls of galaxies, endless lights that spun on and on. Moss, thick and soft, deep green and brown, padded the trunks of fallen trees. We leapt over them, moving deeper, and now Dee was calling to me from above.

'Closer!' she said. 'Almost there! They're near – wait. Slow down!'

I kept running, bursting through a thick line of hanging vines like a frantic bird from a cage. The air was filled with mist and spray, cold on my face, sticking my clothes to me.

'Slow down! Watch the cliff!' shouted Dee, and I saw too late that the ground fell away a few feet ahead, heard the roar of water moving fast against rocks, heard Garth shouting to me, jumping up, waving and flailing. I tried to stop but the ground was slick and smooth, wet rock and old leaves. I skidded, was going to fall, was going to go over into the river – then I felt someone grab my arm, hard and with a sudden strong tug. I lurched backwards, falling down, and then Danny was beside me, his eyes wide and frightened.

'What the hell were you doing?' he shouted. I coughed and looked around, slightly dazed, and then a spurt of anger took hold of my tongue.

'You absolute moron! What was *I* doing? What the hell were *you* doing? Why are we here? Why would you choose now to come back here?'

My arm hurt where he'd grabbed me. My butt hurt where I'd fallen. Danny winced as he pushed himself up, his jeans covered in grass stains and mud.

'You didn't have to follow.'

'Didn't have to— Damn it, this isn't right, Danny! And you,' I said, rounding on Garth, 'why would you help him? We were just downstairs, you could have at least shouted, called to Dee, something!'

'I didn't let him,' said Danny.

'Oh, Mr Big Shot didn't let Death have a say before frolicking off to dream land? Right.'

'I didn't,' said Danny. His voice was calm and cold, but I knew he was angry now. 'The more time you spend here, the easier it is to . . . see how it works. I didn't give him a choice. I made him bring me here.'

I looked at Garth. He was crouched nearby, a dark shape among dark shadows. He nodded slowly. Dee came closer.

'He forced you? How?'

'I don't know. He made the connection himself, used my power, and here we were.'

We all looked at Danny. He glared at us, then turned away to stare out over the cliff.

'This place . . . ' he said. He rubbed his face, his shoulders drooping. 'It's all I can think about. This place, this World Between. It's all I want.'

'Danny,' I said.

'Last time we came here, I just – I focused, remembered the feeling, and then I thought, y'know, why can't I just feel that again? But with a spectre as the gateway, to get me through. And here we are. Home.'

'This is not home.'

'But – smell that! Breathe in, Phil. What do you smell?'

I stepped closer. 'Spice. Mint. Um ... I don't know. Leaves.'

'Not bus fumes and smoke and chip fat, eh?'

'You like chips,' I said. His back was still to me. He was very close to the cliff.

'I like chips,' he said. 'Know what I don't like? The news. War and bombings and evil. I don't like school. I don't like my career bloody counsellors. I don't want to learn to drive, get some job. I don't like missed adventures, places I'll never go, seeing it all on my phone, like it's just some joke, like they're messing with me.'

'What?' I said, but he waved his hand through the air, brushing my words aside.

'This place isn't for you, though,' said Dee. 'And you have to say goodbye. We're going to leave. Garth and me. We're not going to stay on Earth. We can't.'

'We could explore,' said Danny.

'No.'

'We could be happy here.'

'Oh yeah, regular happy family, we are,' I said. The sound of the water grew louder for a second, a gust of wind shifting the mist, water droplets sticking to my hair.

'It's absolutely beautiful,' he said.

'I know,' I said, 'but it's not real, is it? There's no one here. It's just a . . . hollow place. Right, Dee?'

'Airport terminal,' she said. 'Good to use, not to live in. And not safe, either.'

Danny's voice was small. 'I just wanted to see it one last time.'

I was right behind him now. I put my hand on his shoulder, felt his muscles tense and relax. He looked at me.

'They really have to go back?'

'It's not fair for us to decide, is it? They want to.'

He looked so damn young, like a toddler losing his favourite toy. I wanted to laugh. I wanted to slap him.

'Can we stay a bit longer, though?'

'We have stuff to do,' I said. 'Dee said—'

'One hour,' said Garth. Dee raised an eyebrow and he nodded at her. 'All of us. One hour here, and then – back to get ready for the ceremony, yes?'

'What time was it back at the house? Danny, your parents won't get home, right?'

'Not till late.'

I chewed my lip. 'I guess . . . '

'Just look at this place,' said Danny. 'Please. Come and look. Come on.'

I stood next to him now, looking out across the World Between. The river was wider than I'd expected, a huge white-capped mess of spray and rushing water. On the other side, below us, the woods cleared into open fields and hills, growing into mountains that sat, jagged and raw as broken bone, piercing the few remaining clouds. Twilight stretched the shadows out, blurring edges, distorting colours.

'It's amazing,' I said.

'There's nothing like this,' said Danny. Dee snorted.

'Nothing that you've seen, maybe.'

'Hush,' said Garth. 'Let them enjoy it. Let them explore.'

The stars were growing brighter now, and I reached out and squeezed Danny's hand.

For the next hour we walked, the four of us, through that strange, half-real world. Dee was nervous, full of energy and

241

twitches. Garth followed Danny warily, like an injured dog. We walked ahead of the spectres and took in everything we could. From the top of the gorge we followed the forest, slowly sloping down until the riverbank came up to meet us. The water was cool and frothed where it touched the earth. In the distance a red line of mountains broke against the sky in a jagged, toothy grin. Danny reached down and ripped blades of yellow grass from the soil.

'I love it,' he said. He pointed to the sky. 'And see how . . . big everything is? It makes you feel weird, small but important at the same time.'

'There're no people,' I said. 'No friends or family. You couldn't stay forever. We're lucky to have come, but . . . '

Somewhere nearby a bird was singing, short sharp burst of notes that did not echo.

'You never see them, do you?' said Danny. 'Only hear them. Huh.'

'The World Between,' I said.

'Yeah.'

'Are you . . . are you going to promise you won't sneak back here before we say goodbye to them?'

Danny played with the grass between his fingers. 'Yes,' he said, but he didn't look at me.

I nodded. There was dust in the air. 'Good. Well, that's good.'

'Where is this place, do you think?' said Danny. 'Another planet?'

'I don't know stars. I couldn't tell.' I craned my neck to look up. 'That might be Orion's Belt, right there?'

'I don't know. I don't think this is a planet, though. It's a different kind of thing altogether.'

'It's magic,' I said, looking out across the darkening water.

'Yeah. Yeah. That's it. Magic. That's what it is.'

'We should go,' said Dee. She was sitting with Garth a little behind us, her back to the trees, her face lit by the light from the sky.

'OK?' I asked Danny. He shoved me a little.

'I'm not a little kid,' he said. 'I'll be fine. Really. Come on.'

We walked over to the others. Garth took Danny's hand, their eyes meeting and neither looking away. Dee reached out for mine.

'I'm glad you guys liked this place,' she said.

'Me too,' said Danny, and he closed his eyes, and the world went dark.

I gasped, air rushing into my lungs as if I'd been drowning. I felt Danny jerk awake next to me, then bend forward coughing. My vision blurred, and I groaned as I swung my legs to the floor and leaned forward, head in hands. Danny pushed himself off the bed.

'Water,' he said, and he left the room. I heard him heading back down the stairs.

'He'll be OK, right?' I asked. Dee and Garth shrugged.

'He has to be now, doesn't he?' said Garth. I looked at the clock on Danny's bedside table.

'Yeah. OK. Look, we should get going. We need to buy chalk and . . . just get ready.'

Dee's eyes crackled with light.

'It's going to be one hell of a party,' she said.

FOURTEEN

'IT'S BLOODY freezing!'

'Well, what do you want me to do about it?'

'Nothing, I just . . . I just hadn't realised.'

We stood on the pier, the waves rolling beneath us, the ancient wood, scarred and smooth, creaking in the gloom. The last of the sunlight was fading fast, muddying the ocean, nothing more than a dribble of colour lapped up and lost. Clouds hung motionless in the sky, like stuck-on wisps of cotton wool on a child's picture of the stars.

'Good,' said Dee. 'Moonlight won't be a problem. Looks like it's a half moon. Should be strong enough.'

Danny sniffed and rubbed his nose. 'Which is waxing and which is waning? I can never remember.'

'Waning means going away. Getting smaller,' I said.

'Oh. Fitting, that.'

I shivered and hugged myself. Getting on to the pier was easier than I'd thought. It was gated off, the building condemned, but the fences were thin and easy to climb, the street by the pier quiet and untroubled. There weren't any alarms. It probably didn't occur to anyone that someone would try to get in here. Still, we were wary, trying to move quickly, whispering and shushing each other, ducking down when we saw the lights of a car pass by. Now we were looking down the length of the walkway, the buildings – boarded up and left to die – raised up like mountains against the sky beyond. To the left the beach was sandy, popular with families when the weather was warm. To the right the coast was rocky, turning to cliffs and jagged stones, home to seabirds and wild nature. The pier jutted out, one last tooth in the mouth of an old man. It made me feel sad and alone. The ocean roared and the air flicked my hair.

'Right,' said Danny. He was fiddling with a stick of white chalk, the tips of his fingers already dusty and dry. Garth stood next to him, Dee just behind us, and they all looked at me. I cleared my throat.

'Um. This is OK, right?'

Dee nodded. 'We'll be alone. We can form the circle. There's light. We have the book, and the way back. It's amazing. You've actually done it.'

'Not yet,' said Danny.

'Almost.'

'What if we can't?'

'We'll help you,' said Garth. 'OK? It's time. It's finally time.'

Danny looked at his feet, spinning the chalk, blowing out his cheeks. Then, 'OK!' he said. 'Come on. Let's do this.'

He marched forward, his footsteps shaking the board-walk. I followed him, watching my steps, making sure the planks were solid. My cheeks stung from the cold and I dug my hands deep into my pockets. Already, in some unnoticed moment, the sun had finally set. Night washed over the ocean and I looked back to the shore, to the town and its lights, with a cold nervousness.

'Worried?' said Dee.

'Well . . . '

'You act like you haven't summoned Death before.'

'Oh, y'know – just not on a pier. That's all. I prefer my occult ceremonies on dry land.'

'Where's the fun in that?'

'Good point.'

Danny and Garth were getting further ahead of us, heads down as they walked into the wind.

'He's going to be OK, right?' I said. A wave hit the pier's feet and a deep shudder ran through the wood.

'He will be, I think,' said Dee. 'There's enough wonder here as it is. He just needs to know that.'

'Wonder. Right. Good.'

'You don't believe me?'

I laughed, kicking at a mess of dried seaweed and litter that rolled along the planks. 'Oh, no, this place is the bomb.'

'You know what I mean.'

'Yeah, yeah. I do. He'll be OK. Just needs better friends.'

'You really don't like Paul.'

'How d'you work that out?'

'Tell you what,' she said, lowering her voice, 'I'll see if I can get him a haunting. Maybe a few ghouls.'

I stopped dead.

'You can do that?'

For a heartbeat, maybe two, she looked at me and her eyes shone with power and light.

'No,' she said, 'but wouldn't it be fun?'

I snorted and kept on walking. Ahead, Danny and Garth had stopped alongside the pier's main building. It was an old café, built where an old funfair had been. The windows were boarded up, the doors locked, the roof a deep red dome that came to a single point in the centre. By the time we caught up, Danny had already walked around it, peering through cracks, kicking at the walls.

'This window here,' he said, pointing to a black shape on the right-hand side, 'is the only one where the board's come down. We could get through there, right? Otherwise we'll have to try to break in, I guess.'

I stood on my toes and tried to look in.

'I can get through that,' I said, 'but do you think it's safe? What if you fall and there are needles or something?'

'Garth?'

Garth nodded, a grin on his face, and silently stepped through the wall of the building. For a moment there was nothing but the sounds of the sea, and then he was back, shrugging as he spoke. 'Just a few bricks, some paper, a few tables in the centre. Nothing by the window. You're good.'

Danny nodded. 'Better than a sniffer dog.'

'Oi,' said Garth.

'Got you well trained,' said Dee.

'I'm an immortal natural force!' said Garth. 'Anyway, he asked nicely.'

'Did not.'

'Well, he would have.'

'Pff.'

'If you're done,' said Danny – Garth looked sheepish, but he closed his mouth – 'then I'll go first if that's OK?'

'Be my guest,' I said. 'Any chance to get a view of your ass.'

He stuck his tongue out at me as he started to climb up. With a grunt he jumped, scrabbling a bit to push himself through. Then, swinging his legs down first, he fell into the darkness with an echoing thump.

'All good?' I said.

'Oh, it's lovely in here. I don't know why we don't break into piers more often.'

'I'm coming through,' I said.

'I'll make way then, shall I?'

Another shudder, silent but certain, rippled through the wood as a wave crashed down below. I turned back to look down the walkway, back beyond the metal gates to the lights of the town. The tips of waves shone as they broke on the beach and on the rocks.

'You OK?' said Dee.

'Yeah. Never get a chance to see this view. It's nice.'

'You see? Wonder.'

'Sure. OK, let's go.'

I pulled myself up, bracing my knee on the wall and gripping the sides of the window. I saw Danny further inside the room, the light from his phone casting strange shapes on his face. He raised his eyebrows and watched me awkwardly get my legs over and drop down into the empty café.

'You bring me to the nicest places,' he said.

'Nothing bad ever happened in an abandoned building. It's fine.'

He laughed and shook his head at me.

'Oh, no, nothing at all. You're a bad influence, Philippa.'

'The worst. Come on, help me move this table.'

Together – him pushing, me pulling – we cleared the centre of the room, piling the few remaining tables and chairs along the far wall. The room smelled of dust and rot and stale air. There were birds' feathers in one corner, clumps of seaweed and old crisp packets.

'Bit of a step down from where we first came through, eh?' said Garth.

'Company's improved,' said Dee.

'Gee,' said Danny, giving one last shove to the table he was moving, 'thanks. Maybe next time you come you could try to have actual bodies? Then you could do some work.'

'If there's ever a next time,' said Garth, 'I'll work on it. Promise.'

Danny took a deep breath and coughed once, a sharp noise that ran in the empty space.

'So, chalk,' he said. 'What needs drawing?'

'Here,' said Dee, 'I'll show you. Follow my finger.'

I moved out of the way as she crouched down, guiding Danny in a wide circle around the room. The chalk scratched and juddered on the rough boards, and more than once the stick snapped when pushed too hard. Danny's tongue poked out of the corner of his mouth as he listened, concentrated, drew.

'Light,' he said. 'I need light.'

'Here,' I said, turning my phone's torch towards him.

'Good,' said Dee. 'Now we need to inscribe around it. Philippa, you have the book – can you show Danny the page?'

'Inscribe?' said Danny.

'Write. Not English, though. Here, turn the page – yes, there! See those lines? You have to copy them out along the outside of the circle, all the way round.'

'How did I end up with this job?'

'Less talking, more writing,' I said. 'Look, I have to hold the book and the light! We both have things to do.'

'Just copy it carefully,' said Dee.

Danny bent closer, eyes flicking between the book, its pages thin and faded, and the chalk line marked in the dust.

'What's it even say?'

Dee glanced at the words as he wrote them. 'Oh, you know. General stuff. Things.'

'Garth?'

'It's an invitation to the Other Side to break through here – and then other bits are protections and promises so the whole world doesn't . . . break.'

'It's fine,' said Dee, catching the look that passed between me and Danny. 'You have us. Those idiots in their society could have got it all wrong, but we can't. We know how this works. This is us.'

'We're nothing but professionals,' said Garth, beaming in the dark.

It took another fifteen minutes for Danny to finish copying out the writing, double-checking the chalk circle for breaks or scratches. Dee inspected his work, mumbling to herself, squinting at the book, checking the circle. Cold wind blew through the room, and still the ebb of waves moved below us. Once or twice I thought I heard something else out on the pier, the knock of a footstep, the scrape of metal, but as soon as I turned my head, tried to hear through the noise of the night, it was gone. I was nervous and on edge, my fingers frozen from holding the pages of the book. I crouched down by Danny, watching Dee read and re-read the scribbles on the wood.

'What if someone followed us?' I said.

'Why would anyone do that?'

'I don't know. Isn't this illegal, being here? They could have seen. Or, I don't know, what if Paul—'

'Paul?' Danny's voice was strained, an odd calmness making me stutter.

'No, I was just saying, not necessarily him, but someone—'

'You think he'd have waited and followed us? He had to get back to school. He came to see if I was OK. That's all. He's my mate.'

'I didn't mean just Paul, I meant anyone.'

'Right.'

He was annoyed, and he turned away with a huff.

'I just want to make sure we're careful,' I said. A seagull was calling out on the pier; a flutter of wings *beat, beat, beat* through the air.

'How's it look?' said Danny, raising his voice, calling to Dee. She stood up, kept her eyes on the writing, looked up to us.

'It's good,' she said. 'It's all good. We can do this. It's time.'

A strange spark of tension crackled through the chill. I tensed, Danny stood straighter, Garth punched the air, whooping with excitement.

'Yeah! Yeah!'

Dee laughed, and then she stepped in to the circle and swatted at his head. 'Act your age,' she said, 'and come on, step in.'

'I will,' said Garth, 'but hang on. We can't just ... leave. What about goodbyes?'

Danny's face had gone pale. He swallowed, looked at the floor.

'Goodbyes,' said Dee. 'Right. Don't normally get to— I mean ... Yes, you're right. Philippa—'

'Is it goodbye for good?' said Danny.

'Has to be, mate,' said Garth. He stepped closer, lowering his voice. 'But you've been amazing. Really.'

I felt awkward, like I was intruding on something, and I shuffled nearer to Dee, making sure I didn't scuff the chalk.

'Hey,' I said. She smiled.

'Hey.'

'So ... it's been a weird few days.'

'Oh, I don't know. Seemed pretty normal to me.'

'You know you've made me a criminal, now? I mean, we legit broke in to that house, and skived off school, and now we're trespassing here ... '

'There are worse things than a little excitement.'

I raised an eyebrow. 'Like Death?'

'Hmm.'

'I still don't really get what that means. Like, what you are.'

'No, but that's OK, I think.'

'Right.'

'Right.'

Garth was whispering to Danny, something I couldn't hear. They both smiled, but it was sad, and I looked back at Dee.

'We can't really thank you enough,' she said. 'But you've been a good friend, Philippa, for what it's worth.'

'Thanks.'

'That,' said Dee, pointing at the thin book still in my hands, 'is more trouble than it's worth. Destroy it, yeah? Burn it. Throw it in to the sea. Anything. It's not good to have it here in the world.'

I frowned, surprised. 'Destroy it? But you said it's unique! Maybe the only actual book of magic in the world!'

'I did say that, didn't I? Believe me, though, it's best. You know the Society will try again if they get it, and if they don't, someone else will.'

'To control you.'

'To control Death. Sounds mad, I know, but you're young. Older people have a difficult time deciding what's right, and Death – we scare them most of all. They think they can put us in a cage, like a circus lion. Bad idea. Bad for everyone.'

I shook my head. 'I'll get rid of the book,' I said, 'and pretend I know what you mean about anything.'

'Probably for the best.'

She was looking right at me now, intense and unblinking. I tried to hold her gaze, but something in her eyes, some light or power or certainty, made me look away. I felt a flash, for the first time, of Dee as she might be – huge, ancient, terrible, certain. The young girl in front of me flickered in my mind and I shivered at what was behind it all. I looked away, rifled through the pages of the book.

'So ... what do I do?' I said. I realised Danny was next to me again. In the empty room, his breathing sounded louder than ever.

'There's enough moonlight in here?' he said. 'You said you needed moonlight.'

'The window's enough,' said Dee. 'Everything is ready.'

'Come on, then,' said Danny. 'Let's do it.'

'Hold hands,' said Dee. She and Garth were safe within the circle now, looking at us with expressionless faces. Danny took my hand – his was cold, and I almost pulled away. He flashed me a weak, tired smile.

'No ideas,' he said.

'You'd be so lucky.'

Dee cleared her throat.

'Sorry,' I said.

'Repeat what I say when I tell you. That's the trigger, but we can do the rest. We just need you to light the wick. OK?'

'Yes,' we said. Danny squeezed my hand. My heart was racing, my mouth suddenly dry, my tongue numb. I tasted salt again, heard the crash of waves on the shore, the creak of old wood, the groan of metal fences supposed to keep us out.

'Goodbye,' said Garth. Danny swallowed and didn't reply.

Dee raised her voice, impossibly loud, a noise that crashed and roared around the room. They were strange words, crackles of sound, ancient and forgotten, but they were short, definite, impossible to ignore. Danny leaned in to me. 'On three,' he said. 'One ... '

'Two ... ' I whispered.

'Three.'

We spoke, the two of us, copying the words we didn't understand. They flowed from our mouths and echoed in the air. Garth closed his eyes, breathing deeply, his hands stretched out by his sides, his palms facing us. He winced, cocked his head, turned his ear to hear something silent, and, with a thin smile, opened his eyes.

'Got it,' he said, and then, in a blink, he was gone.

FIFTEEN

T HE LIGHT within the circle was blinding, hissing with blue flames, tearing at the air, scorching the wood where the chalk glowed white-hot. I screamed, fell back, tumbled on Danny's legs. He fell with me, our hands still clasped together. The air was full of noise and dust, of spots of light and flecks of fire. In the circle, black shapes surrounded by moonlight, Dee and Garth stood side by side, their eyes filled with flickering darkness, and they laughed as the power of the storm grew and grew.

'What the hell?' shouted Danny, turning his back to them, half standing over me.

'I don't know!' I shouted. 'Is it working?'

'Bloody hell!'

Then, their bodies were fading into the light, the dark shapes melting and turning into smoke, then wisps, then nothing. Now the circle was nothing but light, and still the wind whipped around us, and the chalk crackled, and the room groaned and swayed.

'They're going!' shouted Danny. 'They're actually going! Phil, we— What? What's wrong?'

I gasped, staring past him, gripping his hand tighter than ever. I pointed desperately, trying to get him to see, trying to warn him, and he frowned in confusion. 'Danny,' I said, my voice a squeak in the storm. 'Danny, look!'

He turned, and then he swore, ripping his hand free from mine so he could stand, his back to the wall, battered by the wind, as one by one the members of the Society climbed through the window, their grinning faces lit up by the flames.

'Damn it!' hissed Danny, spinning around to face the window. Three of them were already through, standing against the far wall, the light from the flames casting dancing shadows across their faces. They were wide eyed, staring at the circle with shock, hunger, fascination. More were climbing through, edging forward, until finally a woman – the woman, Susan, the one who led them – stumbled in to the room and stepped forward.

'No!' I shouted. 'Get back!'

'Quiet, girl,' she said. Her voice was calm, businesslike, but her eyes shone with a strange madness, and one of her cheeks twitched as she took in the chalk, the light, the howls of wind.

'Contained it nicely,' she said. 'No offerings, though? We'll have to talk about that.'

'Leave them alone!' Danny shouted. He shifted, raised his fists ready to fight. The woman barely glanced at him.

'Cully,' she said, 'sort him out.'

Someone moved, one of the men, faster than I'd expected. In the room, still flashing with light and dark, still rumbling and cracking, I couldn't see how he did it, but in a second he was beside Danny, a sneer on his face, and then Danny lashed out, fell back, raised his hand to his cheek. He doubled over and gasped, retched, and then the man kicked him, a hard, whip-fast stab. I screamed, stepped forward, but someone was holding my wrists, pulling them tightly, and bursts of pain made me turn, made my eyes water. They were holding me, pinning me against the wall, my arms twisted behind my back.

'Danny! Danny!'

He looked up at me. His face was pale, and a trickle of blood ran from his lip to his chin. I screamed again, pushed against the wall, and then someone slapped me, hard and full on my cheek, and whispered in my ear, words that were lost in the whirl of sound.

'Everyone, quiet!' the woman shouted. She laughed, a high, piercing sound that made me wince. She was facing the chalk circle, moving slowly around it, and in her hands she was holding the book. I groaned, tried to turn my head to see Danny again, but they'd moved him, dragged him away from me.

'Clever,' said someone. 'Very clever. Can't have done it alone. Others, you think? Another society?'

The woman turned and looked at me. Her eyes were stone grey, cold and shrewd and clever. 'No,' she said. 'There's something else here. We'll have to find out what later. There's no time. This isn't stable – look, the flames are fading at the edges. We have to stop it, keep it going. How? Could we bind this circle in another?'

'Tricky,' said the man, Cully, who'd taken down Danny. 'But it could work. I've got chalk. Here, we can freeze this, stop it growing or fading, till we know—'

'Let them go home!' I shouted. 'Please, just stop, just let them go!'

My hands were twisted higher up my back and I screamed again, tears in my eyes. The woman looked at me, frowning, then smiled. 'Yes,' she said. 'That's it. "Them". I should have known. Not such a failure last time, was it? My goodness.'

'What's that?' said a woman. 'What do you mean?'

'No time. I'll explain. Cully, draw faster, man! We have to stop this from closing. Where's the boy?'

Another man cleared his throat. 'Here. He's . . . well, he's not moving much.'

A terrible cold feeling, like ice trickling down my throat, filled my stomach. I twisted my head, desperate to see, to find him. He couldn't be – he couldn't be . . .

'What?' snapped the woman. 'My God, Cully, you didn't—'

261

'I never!'

'Let me look,' said someone, and I heard whispering, and the sound of something dragging slightly on wood.

'He's alive,' said a man. 'Out cold. Blimey, Cully, did you have to? He's just a kid.'

'I barely touched him!' said Cully. 'Kids today, you know, they're too soft, they've got no nerve.'

'We'll deal with him later,' said Susan. She cleared her throat and the others watched her nervously.

'This is our chance, my friends!' she said. 'These children have helped us, in the end. I don't exactly know how – though I have my theories, as I'm sure you have yours – but they have opened, right here, the very door we need. We will latch on, and like a line in a still pool, we shall fish for our prize. Death, my friends! Death as our servant! Death as our pet!'

'No!' I shouted. 'You can't, it won't work! It won't—'

I was punched, hard, from behind. My lungs emptied, my throat closed tight, and I fell to the floor, gasping for breath.

'We can do whatever we want!' someone said. 'Stupid girl, don't think you can understand all of this! Didn't know the book had a tracker in it, did you? Not so clever, were you, stealing it away?'

'I blame the schools,' said Cully. 'Soft and silly, these kids.'

'Keep drawing, Cully. Hurry up!'

'Yes, well, it's hard, you know, this language isn't spoken anymore, and I—'

'Quiet, everyone!' spat the woman. 'We must all hurry, and we must all act together. Gather round. Hold hands. Yes, that's right. Prepare the offerings. We can do this, as before. And this time' – she looked at me, a pleasant smile showing the tips of her teeth – 'we won't have any unexpected visitors, and everything will work out very nicely.'

They left me, then, curled on the floor, shaking, bruised, watching as they surrounded the flames, as they stared in to the shapes that hid Garth and Dee, and they began their magic, their stupid, idiotic magic. I tried to sit up, but it hurt too much, and I gasped, my eyes burning, my head pounding. Across the room I could see Danny lying on the floor, his arms by his side, one foot turned on its side, his head turned towards me, the blood dripping onto the floor.

'Danny,' I whispered, 'Danny, Danny.'

They were chanting now, the Society, and the shadows and the moonlight fell and mingled on the walls. My face was burning with anger and pain. 'Danny,' I said, 'don't be dead, please, I swear, just don't be dead.'

That was when it happened.

Danny opened his eyes, and despite it all – despite the light and the dark and the pain and the blood – he winked at me, and mouthed something.

'What?' I said, but he was already moving, jumping to his feet, wincing as he did so. He moved fast, lunging towards the nearest man and gripping him around his waist. They fell heavily, but Danny was already moving, using his momentum to stumble on and take down the next person. He threw his arms around the woman, ploughing his shoulder into her stomach, sending her crashing to the floor. I gasped and pulled myself up, but Danny was already moving again. The others had turned to him, shouting out, grasping for him, but he kicked, punched, barged ahead, and his eyes locked on me. More shouting, and someone screamed, and then Danny kicked out, lifting his foot, the tip of his shoes pointing high, and he brought his heel down hard, scraping the wood, gritting his teeth even as he was pulled away, as his face was battered and beaten by the adults.

'Leave him alone!' I shouted, moving forward. Someone was shouting, repeating the same word over and over, and Danny was gone, dragged down, screamed at, but I could hear him laughing, even as the roar of the flames got louder.

'Broken!' he shouted. 'Broken!'

I kept moving forward, and then I understood, because Danny had done it on purpose. On the floor where he'd scraped his boot – where there should have been chalk, where there should have been an unending circle – was a blank stretch of wood, no more than an inch wide. The circle was broken. The door was open.

The room we were in exploded.

SIXTEEN

THE SOUND was incredible. I was thrown backwards, flying through the air and skidding on the pier, tumbling, turning, screaming through the dark. The air was frozen, the sudden darkness blinding. The waves were louder here, and for a terrifying moment I thought I would fall into the water, but no – I was lying on the pier, maybe twenty feet from where I'd been. All around me pieces of shattered wood fell smoking and smouldering to the ground. There were screams and cries, and a high-pitched crackle, a strange electric buzz that made my skin crawl. I sat up, my eyes adjusting to the moonlight. Where the room had been there was a crack in the air, a ripped wound in the night that bled a strange, pale light. Lightning flashed from it, white and black, and tendrils of something, hands or smoke or something else, flicked back and forth. I pulled myself up, limping forward.

'Danny!' I hissed. 'Danny! Where are you?'

A man was lying face down near me, one of his hands covered in blood. Further along, a woman was clutching her arm, staggering closer, her face white and filled with anger. Someone grabbed my shoulder and I jumped, wheeling round.

'Whoa!' said Danny, flinching. 'Now's not the time. You can punch me later.'

I stared at him. Then, 'I might!' I shouted. 'What the hell were you doing? Are you OK? What the hell is that?'

The pale light was growing now, the rip growing wider. Danny swallowed.

'I don't know. I panicked! I thought, if Dee and Garth can help us, maybe we could . . . but I don't know – I didn't know.'

'This is bad,' I said. I was shivering. 'This is bad, this is bad, this is bad.'

There was groaning on the pier, and someone shouting, swearing, hawking and spitting. The wind moved ashes and embers into the black water.

'You're hurt,' I said.

'Yeah. You too. Bastards.'

'What are we going to do?'

Danny didn't answer. He was staring at the pulsing, roaring light, and then he stepped away, gripping my arm to pull me towards him. The shape was growing, turning solid, and now the tendrils were searching, pawing at the ground, flicking and twitching as they moved, faster and faster.

'Run,' said Danny. 'Phil, we have to run. Run!'

The light and the flames found the man lying closest to them. He was awake now, sat up, a bruise already swelling on his head. His eyes were wide with fear, his mouth open to scream, but then the thing was on him, spitting and sparking as it touched him, and his eyes went dull, his body limp, and then he was surrounded by the light, by the wind, and he was gone.

'Death!' someone shouted, and others screamed. 'Death! Get away!'

The pier was burning now, smoking and cracking, and the whips of fire coming from the broken circle lashed out. One by one they found what they wanted, men and women running, tripping, falling, and then stopping, frozen and lifeless, melting away like shadows in torchlight. I realised I was crying, shaking sobs that made my throat burn.

'It's killing them!' I croaked, and Danny pulled me again.

'Damn it, run!' he said. I moved, desperate to look away, but everything hurt, everything was slow and stubborn, and the wood was suddenly uneven, splintered and unsteady, and I tripped, pulling at Danny's jacket.

'We can't,' I said. 'We can't.'

There was someone behind Danny, I realised. A shape moved in the night and stood behind him, silent and terrible, smirking and afraid.

'You!' I said. The woman didn't even look at me.

'It was going to be so beautiful,' she said. As Danny

turned she swung her hand, knocking him sideways, and he fell hard on his shoulder, rolling up into a ball.

'Stop it!' I shouted, pushing myself up. She laughed again, and her face was pale, her eyes frenzied. She had a cut on her cheek and blood on her fingers.

'You've ruined it, both of you!' she said.

'Get away!' I shouted, and I pushed her, hard, throwing my weight against her. She growled, clawing at my face, pulling my hair, but she fell, knocking her feet against a pile of smoking rubble, and I stood over her and kicked, just once, at her leg.

'You did this!' I spat. 'We just wanted to help them!'

Someone else screamed, and I turned, searching for Danny. He looked up at me, pale and frightened, wincing as he moved, and I felt angrier than ever.

'My friends,' the woman said, 'are dying.'

'You wanted to play with Death!' I said.

'You don't know anything! We just wanted to—'

She stopped, her tongue frozen, her eyes wide and staring. She gasped, and then her head lolled and her eyes rolled. A thin stream of light had found her, grasping on to her neck, and now it pulsed and grew, covering her like oozing lava. I stepped backwards, and then the woman was gone, and the Death-light turned to me, and slowly, unstoppably, reached for my heart.

'No,' muttered Danny, dragging himself nearer. 'No, Phil, you have to get away, don't let it touch you, don't let it—'

He collapsed again, breathing hard. I spun, looking for

a way out, but the light was all around us now, like the bars of a cage that was shrinking every second. The way off the pier was blocked. Below us the ocean rumbled and laughed. I knelt down and tried to help Danny up.

'Who's left?' he mumbled. His words were thick and slurred, and he wheezed as he breathed.

'What?'

'Who's left on the pier?'

I swallowed. 'No one,' I said. He shuddered.

'Gone?'

'They're dead. They all are.'

'Figures. Us too?'

I was crying, and the tears fell from my chin. 'I think so. I'm sorry, Danny. I'm sorry.'

He smiled. 'Me too. Damn. Really thought it was a great plan.'

I pulled him closer to the edge of the boardwalk, our backs pressed against the railings.

'Rugby tackling the Society,' I said. 'Very cool.'

'I liked when you kicked that bitch,' he said.

He coughed, and there was blood on his hand when he took it away.

'This thing better hurry up,' he said, 'or I'm going to die before it kills me.'

I looked around, but there was no way out. The light was only feet away, and it knew it had us, knew that we were trapped. Slowly, the tendrils gathering to form the shape of a hand, it swelled up and reached out for us both. I closed my eyes and turned away.

'Danny,' I said. He squeezed my hand and said nothing.

The flash was so bright that I saw it even without looking. I jumped, and felt Danny next to me. I heard him breathing, and then waves, and the crackle of the pier.

'What?' I whispered, and I opened my eyes. We were still alive, still crouched there, battered and bruised and shivering, as the light moved around us. The sky was black and shone with stars.

'Phil,' said Danny, 'look.'

'What?'

'It's them!'

'What?'

'Them!'

They were standing there in front of us, shielding us from the searching flames. They were side by side, brighter than anything, shapeless and soundless, but it had to be them. Dee and Garth, too powerful to look at, faced the rolling, roaring Death and would not let it pass. The waves of light moved and rippled, and Dee and Garth moved too, back and forth, shimmering and flowing, the faintest outline of a hand or a face still visible as they moved.

'They're still there,' said Danny, 'and they won't let it get us!'

'What are they doing?'

Danny pulled himself up and watched the flashed of light. 'I don't know. Fighting? Talking?'

The pale light was calmer. It hung like thick mist, the shining shapes of Garth and Dee hovering in front of us.

'They're saving us,' I said. I stepped forward, pulling myself free from Danny.

'Please!' I said. 'Please, we don't want to use you, we didn't want you here, we were helping. Please. Please, let us go.'

I felt a cold shiver run down my spine, the hair on my neck and arms tingling. I felt very small and helpless, and I knew, more certainly than anything, that I was being watched by something huge and ancient and powerful. I felt like a mouse hunted by a tiger, a speck of dust falling into a star. I felt how little I mattered to the world, and I knew that something far away, something beyond my control or understanding, was searching me and judging me. I knew then that I was small and alone, and that Death could take my life as easily as I could pick dirt from my coat. I waited, held my breath, and stared into the light, refusing to look away, refusing to close my eyes.

Then, from nowhere and everywhere, words filled my head, an eruption of whispers, a burst of silence that formed into meaning.

Go and live.

I shuddered and turned to look at Danny. I knew by his face, by his eyes, that he had heard it too. The pier shook, and like a tide being pulled back, a wave flowing away for-ever, the light fell back and filled the tear in the sky. Slowly, the shape got smaller, until a single pinprick of brilliant white hung above the broken pier, lighting up the smudged and shattered chalk circle. It flickered, like a dying torch, and then blinked out into nothingness. Danny and I were alone, cold, scared, and surrounded by the dark.

SEVENTEEN

THE BOOK burned, and everything was lost. I might never know where it came from, what it really was. Dee would want it that way, and I owe her my life, I guess, but still – how can a person just pretend to be happy, when they know there's so much out there?

We managed to get away from the pier before the first policemen arrived. The fire brigade did what they could, but the pier's gone, and I felt bad about that. Danny needed a hospital, and we lied about how he got hurt. I don't think the doctor believed us, but it doesn't really matter in the end. Everything seemed so neat, but that made it worse. I was raw and confused and angry and I'd seen those people die. Danny didn't want to talk about it, and so we didn't, for the most part.

Going to school was hard. It all seemed so pointless, the subjects, the squabbles, the stupid things we cared about. I tried to be nicer to Paul and the others, and to let Danny know that

I really was fine with him having other friends. We've been through enough together. I don't think we'll ever lose that.

Three weeks after the pier – after seeing what we saw, knowing what we know – we sat together for lunch. We didn't have a lot to say, but somehow that was fine. I saw Jess across the room, and she smiled, turned back to her book. Danny's eyes shot up when he heard Paul Baxter's voice. He looked at me and shrugged as the guys came over.

'All right Dan!' said Paul. They bumped fists and Paul set his tray down. 'Practice tonight?'

'Yeah,' said Danny. 'Someone has to kick your ass, right?'

They laughed. I smiled. 'Maybe I should come watch,' I said. 'See what all the fuss is about?'

Paul looked at me. 'Sure,' he said. 'Why not? Maybe you could join the team. You'd probably be better than most of this lot.'

'I'm good on the sidelines, thanks,' I said. 'Far too much effort, you know?'

'Right you are,' said Paul, and he picked up his burger, tearing off a chunk. Danny leaned forward.

'You should come,' he said. 'Really. Be great to have an adoring fan.'

'Oh, we're all your adoring fans!' said Scott.

'Oh, shut up,' said Danny, and he took a chip off Scott's plate.

Paul snorted and sipped his drink. 'Anyone's welcome,' he said.

I looked at the boys, at their jostling and fighting. I didn't know what, but Danny had said something to them, and they were leaving me alone. He caught my eye, smiled, and looked away again. *Rugby*, I thought. *What a stupid game.*

'You know what?' I said. 'I will come. It'll be fun.' The guys cheered, and Danny looked happy, and for the first time in a while, I felt happy too.

What we went through changed us. We don't have to worry about who we hang out with, who we share things with. I'll always be there for him, and Danny knows that.

Here's something he doesn't know: I still go to the house, sneaking in when no one is watching, and climbing the stairs, all rickety and dusty. I go at night to look out over the cliffs. I wait until the full moon and pray for a clear night. I feel the air on my cheeks, taste the salt, let myself shiver. I stare at the stars and lose myself in the size of everything. The world is small and the world is big. I don't quite understand it, but that's how things work, isn't it?

It's strange, being all alone in this dying house, staring at the ink-black night. The sea roars and glistens like a broken sky. I wonder if I took a step, reached out and trusted, what other worlds are waiting? There's life beyond death. That has to change how you live, doesn't it? If I could close my eyes and travel through space, I'd float up, up, up, into the endless light, because there's so much out there, so much to see, and I won't let myself feel trapped in this one amazing life. I won't just watch those stars. I'm going to be one. I'll burn bright and dazzle the world, 'cause I know that I can, 'cause there's so bloody much I want to do, to see, to know.

I dream, sometimes, of the World Between. They're happy dreams, full of light and sound. I fly, because I can when I'm there, and I almost touch the edge of the stars. I look out at this weird world, this place that touches everything, and I call into the wind in shouts and whispers.

'Dee! Dee! Dee!'

She doesn't answer. Life goes on, and so do I, off to find everything.